Dedicated to

the men and women who proudly serve in uniform;

Nurses and Soldiers.

THANK you
for your
Service —

MES

Fort Independence

Castle Island Park

South Boston, MA

CASTLE ISLAND PARK - SOUTH BOSTON, MA

Dawn spills over Boston harbor as people begin their morning exercise rituals, the crisp air sending puffs of mist with each breath.

A foot is placed in a worn sneaker. A young woman in Lycra running gear stretches against a park bench.

A group of colorful Spandex-clad men remove bikes from the top of a Prius, their cycling shoes tapping against the cold concrete.

A thick metal chain is wrapped around a car tire. A worn leather weight belt is strapped to a waist.

A sinewy older man with leather skin and piercing eyes pops the hood of his frayed USMC sweatshirt over the white stubble of his military crew cut. The leather weight belt surrounds his waist, dragging the chain and car tire behind him, the steel belts beginning to show through.

Head down, tire in tow, he slowly starts to jog through snowy Castle Island park, past the rusted cannons and weathered stone turrets of Fort Independence; an old warrior trudging through Southie's historic decommissioned fortress, both showing their age and signs of former battles.

The young woman in Lycra jogs past. She shakes her head and looks back at the strange man hauling a tire. The pack of cyclists swerve to avoid hitting him, yelling obscenities in his direction. The old man just plows right through, a sly smirk on his face.

"Morning Jackie Boy," puffs an approaching jogger. The old man doesn't say a word. A squirrel darts across his path. Jackie stops dead in his tracks. All clear, he continues his daily mission, his focus never wavering. He doesn't see the cyclists. He doesn't see the joggers. He doesn't see the two men in an oversized dark Chevy Chrysler following him from a distance, snapping pictures in his direction.

Head down, tire in tow, Jackie Boy plods on.

HOSPICE CENTER

Megan Hayes, an uninhibited, energetic woman without makeup or pretense, steps out into the same crisp bright morning. She pulls a wool coat over her plain light blue nursing scrubs. Her hat is snug tight over the bushy mess of brown curls that she inherited from her mother, and her mother's people, from the hills of Wicklow, Ireland.

She stops at a newsstand for the Boston Herald newspaper and slides it under her arm. The headline reads: **DIGITRON SALE CONFIRMED. SHARES TRIPLE.** The clerk smiles good morning like clockwork and hands her the usual - bagel, coffee and a bright red carnation.

Megan spots a semi-conscious homeless man propped against the building and squats down to check his pulse and vital signs. She decides he's fine; just asleep from another night of bad luck, bad booze and bad choices.

She lays the Herald over his legs for warmth, places the bagel within reach and pins the red carnation to the lapel of his worn overcoat.

"Promise me you're gonna eat something, Manny," she tells him. Manny grunts and gives a humble nod. Satisfied, Megan continues on her way to visit patients.

QUINCY, MA

The Wallace house is a charming well-kept saltbox colonial in the Wollaston Beach section of Quincy just south of Boston. The house is large and inviting, handsomely landscaped with trimmed bushes now covered by green plywood and brown burlap to protect them from the harsh South Shore winters. It's a neighborhood where the homes are old and stately, and the air is clean and full of the nearby sea. There's a kind of mellowness and memory of another time and another America.

Megan walks along the sidewalk and up the short asphalt driveway. She turns the lock (since she comes and goes at all hours, most of the families in her care will give a spare key) and enters a home that is immaculate but dated. The furnishings look brand new, as if they were just brought home from Jordan Marsh - in 1978. Mrs. Wallace is a woman who appreciates the daily graciousness of life, so the Waterford crystal and China tea cups are always set, waiting for use in her dark paneled dining room.

Megan walks up the Oriental carpeted stairs to Mrs. Wallace's bedroom, draping her coat and hat on an embroidered wingback chair sitting by the door.

The bedside nightstand is covered with pill bottles and a gallery of family pictures. Megan picks up a simple brushed silver frame that has been knocked down. The strong, handsome man in a 1950's black and white photo stares back at her from behind the glass. She dutifully stands the frame back in its rightful place alongside all the others.

Megan peels back the curtains, spilling morning sun into the room. "Good morning, sunshine," Megan cheerily greets her patient.

Genevieve Wallace, a frail elderly woman with a kind, welcoming face that seems to always rest in a smile, lays in her king-sized bed with four oversized white pillows surrounding her thin frame, an embroidered duvet is pulled tightly to her chest.

"Oh, Megan," Mrs. Wallace replies, blinking with confusion as her eyes adjust to the light. "Good morning. What...what are you doing here?"

"I'll be coming full time from now on. Tricia took on a new position at the Center."

"Oh, that's nice," says Mrs. Wallace. Everything is nice to this kind old woman. "It's just, well, you haven't met my son yet. Tricia didn't really get along too well with him. He can be quite a colorful character."

"Oh, I think I can handle colorful characters," Megan says with a confident grin as she begins to wrap a blood pressure cuff around her patient's thin arm.

"Did you knock this picture over?" she asks wondering if Mrs. Wallace tried to get out of bed on her own.

"Oh, that's just Mr. Wallace, he passed a few years ago. I put his picture down at night because he talks too much. Yap, yap, yap all night long."

"Aww, that's nice," smiles Megan. "He misses you."

"He's just horny," replies Mrs. Wallace in a matter of fact tone. Megan busts out a laugh.

"I'm serious," Mrs. Wallace continues. "The man was insatiable. I just want a few more days of peace and quiet before he jumps my bones."

"Let's not talk like that," Megan says, checking the blood pressure, good not great, then looks to the nightstand of family photos. "And who are these beauties?"

"That's my granddaughter and my daughter-in-law," says Mrs. Wallace beaming with maternal pride. She looks over from her pillows with a hint of sadness. "It's hard for them to come by, they have so many activities. But, that's alright. I told Timothy I don't want them to see me like this."

Suddenly, music comes rising from the hallway. It's some sort of island steel drum. Then, bouncing through the door comes Tim Wallace.

"Aloha! Who's ready for Happy Hour?" he cheerily exclaims, his energy filling the room.

The flowered shirt and straw hat on his head make him look much younger than his thirty-eight years. Megan immediately notices his boyish good looks as he Hula dances across the room with an '80's style boom box in hand. She instinctively checks his left hand. Wedding ring. Of course. She already knew that.

"I thought we'd take a trip to the islands today, Mom. Jimmy Buffett and boat drinks," Tim says almost singing the words.

"Oh my, that sounds like fun," says Mrs. Wallace, beaming.

"You must be Tim," Megan says simultaneously standing to introduce herself and straighten her unflattering scrubs.

"And you are most definitely *not* Tricia," replies Tim with a firm handshake, almost mocking the formality of the introduction.

"Timothy. You be nice," commands Mrs. Wallace in a stern 'obey your mother' kind of manner.

"I'm always nice, Ma."

"I mean 'Be nice to Megan,'" she replies.

"I'm always nice, Megan," says Tim, looking straight at Megan, his eyes full of mischief. Megan notices the slight dimple in his cheek when he smiles.

"Well, you weren't always very nice to Tricia," his mother scolds him.

"Awe, she was no fun!" says Tim. He looks at Megan with a wink. "That woman needs a good stiff drink. Or a good stiff something."

Megan stifles a chuckle then tries to regain some kind of control. "I'm here to help with the transition. Could you, ah…could you please turn the music down?"

But Tim isn't paying attention. He's too busy turning the Calypso steel drum music up. Waaay up.

"The 'transition', huh?" he shouts with a mocking tone. "Is that what we're calling it? You ready for the 'transition', Ma?"

Mrs. Wallace gives her son a resigned shrug, "As long as there's music, Timothy. There should always be music."

Megan glances over at her, recognizing that saying.

Tim changes the subject, shouting above the music.

"I didn't miss medication time, did I? That's our favorite part of the day. Well, that and Karaoke. You sing Megan?" he asks, holding a microphone in her face like a game-show host. Megan pulls away, getting annoyed.

"I'm more of a sing-into-a-hairbrush kinda gal. Listen, Mr. Wallace, we need to go over…"

"Tim," he says flatly. "Mr. Wallace was my father."

Megan puts on her nursing face. "Tim. Your mother doesn't need any stress. We need to go over procedures and…"

But Tim doesn't pay attention. He's too busy wrapping a Hawaiian flowered lei around his mother's neck. "She doesn't seem stressed to me. You stressed, Ma?"

Mrs. Wallace appears delighted with her son's antics. Then, to Megan's complete and utter shock, Tim begins to unravel a plastic beer funnel.

"What...what are you doing?!" asks 'nurse in charge' Megan Hayes.

"Any way we can get the medicine in, right Ma?" he says. He turns to Megan, "You should have been here last week for Shoe Shots. I thought Tricia was gonna blow a gasket."

"Well, it is more fun this way," says Mrs. Wallace, smiling sheepishly as if to ask Megan for approval. But Megan's attention is now fully on Tim. "This is all against protocol. It's unsanitary and not safe and..."

Tim looks at her blankly. "What are you, the 'Fun Police?'"

Megan is taken aback. 'Jesus,' she thinks to herself. 'Against protocol? Did I really just say that?'

"No," she stammers to answer him. "What? I'm not..."

Mrs. Wallace can sense the tension rising in the room. "Tell me all about the girls, Timothy. What are they up to today?"

"Well, for starters, Olivia wants to get a cat," he replies.

"Oh, that's nice. Isn't that nice, Megan?"

"They'll love it," says Megan.

"Ugh, I hate cats," growls Tim.

At least Megan can agree with him on this one. She is definitely a dog person.

"But I'm being overruled...again," says Tim reaching into his back pocket. "Here, Livy drew you another picture, Ma. I'll put it on Dad's closet," he says and begins to tape the colorful drawing alongside several others.

"We were just talking about your father," says Megan, trying to work her way back into the conversation.

"He was insatiable," quips Mrs. Wallace offhandedly. Tim looks back. "Huh? What was that...?"

"*Irreplaceable,*" says Megan quickly. "She said your father was irreplaceable."

She approaches Tim and hands over a business card. "I told your mother I'll be coming full time now. You and I are going to have to find a way to work together. Here. This card has my cell number."

Tim shoots her his boyish smirk, the dimple almost singing to her. "You always give your number to strange men?"

She shoots a smirk back. "Guy in a Hawaiian shirt giving medication through a beer funnel? What's so strange about that?"

He laughs and takes the card with a smile.

****

Megan stands inside the plexiglass bus stop staring at her reflection. 'Great first impression,' she thinks to herself reviewing the unflattering blue nursing scrubs. 'And what the hell was with all that protocol bullshit?'

Posted on a wall beside her is a billboard of a happy, skinny model frolicking on a beach. Megan flips her the bird and boards the bus.

She finds a seat in the back, alone, and quietly begins to scan the advertisements above the bus windows. Dating Services. A couple having a romantic dinner. 'Royal Caribbean' cruises with perfect families on their perfect vacations. Jesus, it's never ending.

The morning commuter traffic builds up as the bus slows to a stop. A sinewy old man boards, bumping and clamoring his way up the three steps carrying a weight belt, tire and chain. Megan slouches and pulls a nearby newspaper over her face.

"An 'N' and a 'G'?" Jackie Boy growls looking at the Asian bus driver's ID badge. "Don't they have vowels in China?"

"What happened, Jackie Boy," replies Ng the driver. "You lose the three other tires from your car?"

"Mexican stole them," Jackie replies sharply. "Say, how can you drive with your eyes half shut?"

"How can you walk straight, ya drunk Irishman," Ng snaps back, the banter part of their daily routine. He motions Jackie to move in. "Get behind the yellow line."

"Said the yellow driver," Jackie mumbles over his shoulder.

Megan peeks over the paper, skulking deeper in her seat as Jackie Boy maneuvers the wet tire through the crowded bus. He stands beside a young woman with her arm full of groceries, her hand holding tightly to the strap overhead. The bus jolts forward, causing them to have an awkward bump encounter. Three rough looking teenagers sitting side-by-side begin to snicker.

Jackie Boy sees them and yells. "Hey!" The teenage punks are heads down. "You three!" he continues, finally getting their attention. "You're supposed to give up your seat for a lady."

"I ain't standin' the whole ride home," says the first punk, trying to be the toughest and the leader.

Jackie growls back. "You'll stand, or else you won't be able to stand."

Megan, still hiding behind her paper, rolls her eyes.

"Go away old man before you piss yourself," says the punk, laughing along with his friends. Ng looks up in his rear-view mirror.

"Didn't anyone teach you manners, boy?" growls Jackie.

The punk stands up and approaches.

"Who you callin' boy, old man?"

"You're certainly not a man, '*boy*'," says Jackie, punching the word. "A man gives up his seat for a lady."

The teenage punk approaches and holds a finger in Jackie's face. "You best keep your mouth shut."

Jackie doesn't flinch. With a snake quick motion, he grabs the kid's wrist and twists. The teenager's sidekicks jump to his rescue, but Jackie twists harder.

"No! Stop!" the punk screams, writhing on his knees in agony. Jackie Boy addresses them all calmly, politely, as if he were a Science teacher conducting an experiment in front of class.

"Now. If I just apply the slightest bit more pressure, I could snap this wrist in two. Wouldn't that be a goddamn shame? No more video games. No more texting. No more pointing at people trying to teach you about manners and respect."

Jackie smirks and twists harder. More pain. Big time. The teenager moans. Jackie leans close, looks at the teenager with cold hard eyes, and growls in a lower, more frightening octave.

"Or maybe I'll just keep you in this position until you piss yourself."

Tires screech and the bus comes to an abrupt stop. Ng yells, "Jackie! That's enough."

****

Two figures stand side-by-side on the sidewalk as the bus pulls away.

"Do you ever make it to our stop without getting kicked off?" asks Megan.

"It's rare," replies Jackie Boy.

"You're amazing, Dad."

"I've been told that," says Jackie Boy as he picks up his tire, weight belt and chain.

"I met your mother on a bus, ya know," he says, hauling the tire by his side.

"I know," replies Megan, her boots stepping on the frozen snow. "She told me you twisted her arm until she'd go out with you."

"Old habits," replies Jackie.

Father and daughter turn to make their way home.

SOUTH BOSTON

So much has changed since Jackie Boy grew up on the Irish-American streets of South Boston, affectionally known as 'Southie.' Today the area is the most sought-after gentrified real estate in Boston. Yuppies, Gen Xers and Millennials are taking over the traditional working-class neighborhoods, splitting two-family and triple-decker houses into individual condo units. Not Jackie Boy. He's not budging. It's His House. And His Town.

There's a toughness to the people of Southie. Street tough. Maybe it was from the years of busing in the 1970's when the city forced school integration onto the poorest sections of the area. Or maybe the toughness and resilience stems from the Irish in them. The people of South Boston have a proud look, one that's always ready to bust a laugh or bust your balls. Megan may have inherited the curly brown hair from her mother, and the stubbornness from her father, but she got her street toughness from the good solid people of Southie.

Jackie and Megan walk up M Street, past rows of meticulous two-family houses that stand shoulder-to-shoulder along a tree-lined, snow-covered road. They stop in front of their Kelly green two-family. Jackie Boy's military training and work ethic always made sure the home was run in an orderly fashion, and his oversized ego made sure that it's the best-looking house on the street.

He points to a row of bird feeders hanging along the front porch.

"Can we finally get rid of these things? There's shit everywhere. And they attract rats."

"They're not rats, Dad," replies Megan. "They're squirrels - and you know Mom loved to feed them too."

Jackie grumbles as they climb the stairs.

"Ungrateful little rodents."

****

Ornate crown moldings wrap along the ceiling and up the dark oak stairway of the Hayes entryway. It displays the craftsmanship and attention to detail of a bygone era; a reflection of the man who originally built the house in 1928, and of the man who has meticulously maintained it for the forty-three years since Jackie bought it.

The living room is filled with strong, heavy furniture put together by tools - real tools - used by the hands of men, not flimsy prefab yuppie pieces assembled with Ikea wrench keys.

Jackie Boy leans his tire by the front door, plops into his sturdy La-Z-Boy recliner and clicks on the rerun of last night's Bruins game.

"I don't like you jogging through the park," Megan yells from the adjacent kitchen. "Can you go somewhere else? Like a gym, maybe?"

"Negative," Jackie snaps, then says to no one in particular, "Castle Island's gettin' crowded. All those Goddamn yuppie bikers with their neon shirts and grape-smuggler shorts. It's just riding a bike, for Chrissake. Sweatpants and a sweatshirt work just fine. What's with the costume?!"

Megan peeks her head around the corner from the kitchen and looks at her father in his mangy sweatpants and faded USMC t-shirt.

"But you look perfectly normal in that get-up dragging a tire," she quips.

"That's how we trained in the Corps," he barks.

"I'm sure you did a lot of crazy things when you used to be a Marine," she says cracking eggs into a pan.

Jackie Boy's face turns red with anger. "Hey, Missy. I didn't *use* to be a Marine. I *am* a Marine!"

Megan rolls her eyes. She knows the drill. The Corps runs through her father's bloodstream and affects his every action, every decision, every emotion.

"At ease," she says setting plates on the Formica kitchen table. "It's not about the park, Dad. It's about being safe. I'm sure there are rules against dragging a tire all over the Castle Island."

Jackie mumbles, "What are you, the 'Fun Police'?" Megan's head pops out again.

"What? What did you say?"

Jackie ignores her and stays tuned to the Bruins.

She brushes off the familiar remark. "It's supposed to snow later. We're gonna need somebody to shovel the walk."

"I'm 68 years old and can bench press 300 pounds," replies Jackie as a statement of fact. "I can shovel my own Goddamn stoop, thank you very much."

"You throw your back out again you'll be laid up for weeks. The people at Firestone tire would be devastated," Megan quips.

"Ha ha. Very funny," Jackie replies.

Megan finishes setting the table and lights the two candles that are set in the middle. She thinks for a moment as reminiscent smile reflects off the small flames, then shakes off the memory.

"I'll check with Loretta tomorrow," she says. "She told me Michael could use something to do after school."

"I'm not paying him," snaps Jackie Boy. "Did you know on his 70th birthday Jack LaLanne pulled 70 rowboats across Long Beach Harbor. With his teeth!"

Megan enters the room. She can see her father's wheels turning. "Don't even think about it, Marine. Keep it up and you'll end up back at the Carney in traction. Let's go. Breakfast."

He doesn't move. Eyes on the TV, he replies, "after this period."

She gives a cold hard stare. Jackie does his best not to make eye contact then starts to plead. "We're down 3-2. Can't I eat breakfast in my own house in front of my own TV?"

"Let's go," she demands. "Mom's rules."

Jackie still doesn't budge. Megan's voice rises. "Now!"

For a tough, hardened Marine, Jackie Boy is terrified of strong women. He leaps out of the Lay-Z-Boy like a frightened child and rushes to his seat at the kitchen table.

Megan walks over to the adjacent living room and approaches what may possibly be the one thing Jackie Boy loves more than his wife, more than his daughter, maybe even more than the Marine Corps itself; shelves lined with his prized collection of vinyl record albums and 45's. It's an eclectic assortment from the 1950's and '60's with classic artists like Dean Martin, Johnny Mathis, Nat King Cole, Patti Page, and Perry Como. This is the music Jackie Boy grew up with; softer music from a simpler time. His is a generation raised on 'good war and good music' as Jackie would say, as opposed to Megan's generation of 'bad war and bad music'.

Megan slides an LP from its sleeve. "Careful there, Missy," commands Jackie Boy watching closely as she gingerly, *carefully* drops the needle onto the spinning record. After a pop and a scratch, Tom Jones begins to croon THE GREEN GREEN GRASS OF HOME.

Down the road I look and there runs Mary
Hair of gold and lips like cherries

It's good to touch the green, green grass of home

"There now. Isn't this nice?" says Megan as she sits at the table, the candles flickering between them.

"Candles with breakfast?" says Jackie. "Don't you think this is a bit much?"

"You know Mom's rules. 'Candles at the table, and music. There's should always be music,'" replies Megan.

Jackie nods and smiles. It's a sad reminiscent smile.

"This guy, Tom Jones. He was one of her favorites, ya know. I always thought he was a big sissy. Women throwing underwear at him on stage."

"You're just jealous," says Megan. "You think everyone who isn't a Marine is a big sissy."

He gives her a look that says, 'am I wrong?', then reaches for the salt shaker. Megan smacks his hand. "Ah-ah-ah, Mr. Healthy. No salt."

"Jesus," he pleads. "I can't have salt. I can't eat in front of the TV. I can't shovel. I need to get my own Goddamn place."

"You need to get a job, is what you need. Give you something to do all day instead of pulling that silly tire all over Southie."

"Sure," Jackie replies dripping with sarcasm. "Maybe I can hand out smiley stickers at Walmart."

Megan looks at a wicker basket in the corner of the counter overflowing with a stack of bills. "Maybe I should fill out an application myself," she quietly mutters to herself.

"You're wound too tight," says Jackie shoveling down a mouthful of unsalted eggs. "You don't need a second job. You need to get laid."

Megan punches his arm. "Eww, stop that! No men for a while. I'm thinking about getting a cat."

"Ugh, I hate cats," he growls sounding exactly like Tim Wallace. He continues to devour his tasteless meal. "So, that old lady kick yet or what?"

"Stop it, Dad. No."

"Yea, well, I wouldn't buy her any green bananas, if you know what I mean."

Megan rolls her eyes. "There's that sweet compassion I grew up with. You're impossible."

"It's this hospice thing. It makes you all creepy. You used to nurse people back to health. Now all your patients are in God's on-deck circle. It's depressing, for Chrissake."

"I need to be there, Dad," she tells him. "Nobody should be alone when they die."

Megan immediately regrets that. Jackie abruptly stops eating and lays down his fork. A cold, uncomfortable silence hangs over the table.

"I...I'm sorry. I didn't mean it like that," she says. Jackie Boy says nothing, then tries to shrug off the remark.

"Everyone dies alone, Megan."

"Yeah, well, not on my watch," she states firmly. Her look says she means it. Jackie Boy tries to lighten the mood of the room.

"Well, Marines don't die without orders, so we better get used to being roommates."

With that, he props an elbow up on the table, challenging his daughter to arm wrestle. She plants her hand firmly in his.

"No crying when you lose."

"I didn't cry last time!" he fake whines.

"Ready?" she says. "Three. Two. One. Go!"

BOOM! Jackie Boy's wrist is slammed to the table - and the excuses begin.

"You cheated! My bursitis is acting up. I...I didn't have time to…"

"Go," smiles Megan. "You can watch the highlights."

"Really?" Jackie Boy beams like a ten-year-old.

"Yeah. Bruins lost 4-3," she tells him.

"Aww, come on!"

He regains his military composure and asks, "You, ah, want some help policing the kitchen?"

Megan gives him a cocky but daughterly smirk.

"I got this."

Jackie Boy stands tall, eyes front, shoulders back, and snaps her a smart salute.

"Permission to leave the table, Ma'am?"

Megan smiles at their formal tradition. "Permission granted."

Jackie gently winks, "Semper Fi, little girl," then excitedly heads to the living room.

Megan sits alone at the table and stares at the flickering dinner candles. She slowly removes a pill bottle from her hospital smock pocket and twirls slowly it in her hand.

Across the street, the oversized Chevy Chrysler is parked in the shadows. Two men snap long-range photos of Megan through their car window.

HOSPICE CENTER

The lunchroom table is a cluttered mess of coffee cups, donut boxes, local papers and magazines. Davey Devaney, an overtly gay and totally comfortable-in-his-skin Social Worker, sits sifting through a pile of invitations for his upcoming wedding.

Sitting beside Davey is Loretta Evans, the anointed maternal nurse of the Hospice Center. Her dark skin is devoid of makeup and her almond-colored eyes convey a tenderness and a knowledge of things that most fellow nurses haven't even learned yet. Loretta has the air and attitude of a woman comfortably settled into her wisdom and sense self. She might as well wear a shirt that says, 'Do Not Fuck With Me Today.'

"Seriously?" she says reviewing Davey's guest list.

"I had to. She's our boss now, remember?" Davey replies, full of bite and sarcasm.

Megan enters the room and shakes the snow from her jacket and boots. "Good morning, guys. It's really coming down out there." She looks to Loretta. "You think Michael could help shovel me out at home?"

Davey gasps. "You must be kidding. You actually think Jackie Boy's gonna let someone help?"

"I know, right?" replies Megan, hanging up her coat. There's a familiarity between these two friends that goes unspoken. "That man's stubbornness is a work of art," she continues. "He throws his back out again he'll be laid up for weeks. Can you imagine him missing a workout?"

Davey shivers with mock terror at the thought.

"My Michael sits alone all afternoon playing them video games," says Loretta. "And the eating. He's starting to get teased at school about his weight." She shakes her head with concern and looks at Megan. "The boy's been a mess ever since Carl left. I think it'd be good for him to have some chores."

"Speaking of sons," chimes Davey, "How'd it go at the Wallace's?"

Megan shakes her head and rolls her eyes. "Her son had me administer medication through a beer funnel. Can you believe that? Mrs. Wallace called him a 'colorful character'. I think he's just plain nuts."

"He sounds fun," says Davey, as he cheerily licks invitation envelopes.

"Mmmm, hmmm," nods Loretta with approval.

"He's irresponsible, that's what he is," says Megan. "Childish. Unsanitary. Immature."

Davey looks at Loretta. "I think she likes him."

Megan just glares.

"Would you listen to yourself?!" Loretta pipes up. "You sound like Tricia." Davey shudders as if a cold wind just blew through the room. 'Jesus,' thinks Megan, 'Maybe I am turning into the Fun Police.'

"Is he handsome?" chirps Davey.

"Relax. He's married," she replies. "And next week you'll be married to Kevin."

Loretta pipes in, mindlessly stuffing envelopes for Davey. "Half of all marriages today end in divorce. That gives you a 50/50 shot that he's gonna be available eventually."

"Why does everyone think you need a man to be happy," asks Megan, seriously meaning it.

"Everyone *I* know does," Davey deadpans.

Megan sits down and begins to scan through the clutter of papers.

"I think I'll just get a cat."

"Uh, uh. No way," snaps Loretta, pulling the papers away. "I'm not gonna let you turn into one of them crazy white ladies with thirty cats."

"I said *a* cat, Loretta. One," says Megan, then adds sadly, "at least I'd have something."

Davey and Loretta look at each other as if preparing to lecture her, but Megan stops them before they even start.

"No. Stop. No 'Joe lectures' today. We're done. And I'm *fine* with it. Really," she says trying to convince her friends - and herself. But they know she's not fine. It's just her defense mechanism. Trying to be all 'Southie tough.'

Loretta speaks up. "Look, I was devastated when Carl left me for that trashy cashier at Market Basket. But my ninety-two-year-old grandmother gave me some advice that changed my life. She said, 'there's only one thing you can do to feel better...'"

"What's that?" asks Megan.

"'Go bang his best friend!'" says Loretta, blasting a laugh. "And I did too!"

"Yahtzee!" shouts Davey, raising his hands in the air and giving Loretta a high five.

Megan smiles at her friends. "Well, Joe's best friend was Kevin ...and he's banging Davey now."

"Double Yahtzee!" shouts Davey. High fives all around as they roar with laughter.

The lunchroom door swings open and all the air is suddenly sucked from the room because in walks Tricia Coughlan, their portly supervisor, perfectly coiffed in a stiff, starched outfit that matches her stiff, starched personality. Her face is bleached like corn starch, the whiteness in stark contrast to the black hair she has pulled tightly into a bun which seems to literally tug at her face.

"David, why are you always here? Social Services is on the third floor," she says with her permanent face of contempt.

"Can I help it if I'm so social?" Davey smartasses. Megan and Loretta giggle like little girls.

"Well at least this will save me a trip upstairs. Even though I am opposed to gay marriage, I feel it's my duty as your newly appointed manager to support the staff. Edward and I will be attending your 'occasion'," says Tricia, her voice registering her level of disapproval.

"It's a 'ceremony', Tish," Davey corrects her. "Chicken or fish?"

"We would prefer to bring our own pre-made meals, thank you very much," she curtly replies. "And it's Tricia, not 'Tish'. It's short for Patricia."

Not really giving a shit, Davey snorts, "Well, I'm sure your husband will see something there he likes." The hint of sarcasm in his voice is evident only to Loretta, and they both stifle a laugh.

Tricia tries to gain control of the room. "There have been recent discrepancies in the dispensary and Management wants to review procedure. There will be a mandatory team meeting at 5:30 in the conference room."

"Discrepancies?" says Loretta full of attitude and clearly upset by the accusation. "What the hell is that supposed mean?"

"That's a fancy word for 'someone is stealing drugs," quips Davey.

Megan looks at her co-workers with a reassuring, cocky smirk that they all know says, 'I got this.'

"Well, you're the one in charge of procurement now, Tricia," Megan reminds her in a classy yet condescending tone. "Why do you need us to be there?"

"It's a *mandatory* Team Meeting, Megan. And yes, you are right, I am in charge now. I'm giving up dinner with my *husband* to be there," says Tricia making sure she punctuates the word 'husband'. "Unless, of course, you have someone else you need to be with tonight?" she says to Megan with a cold glare.

Megan's fist begins to clench as a cold, frosty silence covers the room.

Tricia speaks first and continues to assert her delusional authority. "I didn't think so. I trust things went well at the Wallace's?"

"Perfect," says Megan with pissy curtness. "Just perfect. All according to standard procedure."

"Did, uh…did Mrs. Wallace ask for me?" asks Tricia, trying not to appear overly interested in the answer.

"No. She didn't," replies Megan flatly.

"Oh. Ok. Fine," says Tricia, masking her disappointment. "Well, I'll see you all at 5:30. Sharp."

With that, Tricia grabs the last donut, turns and leaves the lunchroom.

Loretta leans over and puts her hand over Megan's tightly clenched fist. "OK now. Let's settle down, Sweetie."

"Why does she hate me so much? I swear, if I didn't need the money so bad I'd quit this place in a heartbeat."

"Please, this place *is* your heartbeat," says Loretta in her maternal soothing tone, still trying to loosen Megan's tight grip. "And listen, Tricia doesn't hate you. She hates what you have."

"What I have?" replies an exacerbated Megan. "Oh, I'm just living the dream here. Thirty-six. Single. Living at home with my crazy ex-Marine father..."

Loretta and Dave shudder.

Megan corrects herself. "I know. I know. He *is* a Marine - but a crazy Marine, who drags a tire all over Southie and thinks he's gonna live forever. What was it you said I have again?"

Loretta looks her friend in the eye. "You have a sense of confidence. A sense of caring. A sense of humor. Tricia believes she'll never have any of those things."

Megan sighs and rubs her now unclenched hand.

"Yeah, well, at least she believes in *something*," she says looking off with a hint of resignation. "Maybe I'll just marry one of the Eastie 'Goombah' boys."

Davey throws all ten fingers to his cheeks. "Mamma Mia! Now those are four spicy meat-a balls!"

GIORDANO HOUSE- EAST BOSTON

The smell of garlic bread and simmering marinara sauce

wafts through the air in East Boston's ethnic Italian

neighborhood. Like many of the areas with proximity to

Boston, gentrification has taken hold of neighborhoods trying

to retain their old school traditions and charm. Old men still

play bocce ball. Women buy their fruit at the corner stands.

Bathtub Virgin Marys proudly adorn front yards, silently

standing holy sentry over homemade gardens awaiting the spring thaw.

Just as South Boston is known locally as 'Southie', East Boston was given the clever label of 'Eastie'. The Celtics, Red Sox, Bruins and Patriots may have racked up a few Championships over the years, Boston won't be winning any awards for clever or original town nicknames.

Hospice Nurse Megan Hayes enters a kitchen full of food, noise and chaos. The ceiling is yellowed over the stove from years of cooking and simmering red tomato gravy. (God forbid you call it sauce around here!)

A long table is overflowing with Italian food. Antipasto. Baked eggplant. Three kinds of pasta. Chicken Parmigiana. And bread. Lots and lots of bread. You get the impression this could be Thanksgiving, but it's just another Tuesday night supper at the Giordano house.

Marco, Silvio, Bruno and Stevie, four chubby tattooed, spiked-haired Mama's-boy's in their 30's, cook and argue and dip bread into the 'gravy' and argue and yell and eat and argue some more. They are stereotypical and interchangeable with heavy Italian mannerisms - in other words, stand back when they start talking because you might get knocked out with a swing of their hands.

They stop what they are doing (arguing) to greet Megan.

"Yo Meg."

"How you doin', kid?"

"Hey. How you doin'?"

Marco, the oldest, yells towards the stairs, "Yo, Ma! The nurse is here!"

Silvio is busy stirring the gravy, and remarks. "It's her expiration date.'"

Megan nods, thinking to herself, 'Expiration Date.' That's pretty good. Never heard that one before.'

Bruno, the smarmiest of the bunch, puts his chubby tattooed arm around her. "So, Meg, you gonna go on a date with me or what? I'm thinkin' a little wine. A little pasta. A little sponge bath."

Megan flashes a teeny-weeny inch sign with her fingers. "I'm thinkin' a *little* somethin' alright."

The brothers howl. "Hey!" "Ho!" "Badda Boom!"

Bruno tries to recover, his white tank top splattered in red gravy. "You watch. I'm gonna go put on my classy blue silk shirt. You'll be all over me," he says, and waddles off.

"Hey, that's my shirt, asshole!" bellows Stevie, cutting Scali bread at the table. "You touch that shirt and I'll kill ya dead. Oops. Sorry, Meg."

Megan's not offended. Pretty much ever. Southie-tough.

"Yo, Meg, taste this," says Silvio lifting the ladle from a huge cast iron pot. "You think too much oregano?"

"She's Irish," yells Marco. "Probably uses sauce from a jar."

The boys react hard. "Woah!" "Marone!" Silvio blesses himself.

"Hey Meg, you gonna go on a date with Bruno or what?" asks Stevie. "He really likes you, ya know"

"I don't think so," replies Megan, meaning 'no', as in 'No Way Would She Ever' go on a date with Bruno, or with any of the Giordano boys. She's just trying to be polite.

"What are you...a lesbian?" asks Marco.

"Just waiting for my true love, boys," Megan smiles back.

"Hoh, Snow White over here!" shouts Silvio.

Bruno returns to the kitchen wearing an absolutely hideous blue silk shirt. Megan looks him up and down. Its shiny. And gawdy. And loud. Just like Bruno.

"This is the shirt you two are fighting over?" she asks with biting sarcasm. Bruno beams with pride and puffs his chest. "Pretty sweet, right?"

Megan looks at him in a consoling, tender manner.

"I'm a hospice nurse, Bruno. Seen just about every stage of death. But this?" she says putting an arm on his shoulder. "It's time to pull the plug, big guy."

His shoulders drop. The brothers crack up laughing.

****

Megan enters a room adorned with gold paintings of Patron Saints. Heavy velvet maroon colored drapes hang at the tall windows. Laying in a bed of satin sheets is Maria Giordano, the boy's bigger-than-life Italian Mama. A wonderful woman with deep, dark, loving eyes, arms that resemble over-sized pillows that could both smother you in a loving embrace or snap you in half if you stepped out of line. Her hands are knotted and arthritic from her early years working a sewing machine for Leon Clothing, and from the hours and hours she spent in her kitchen rolling manicotti, pouring pizzelles, and making potato gnocchi.

"How are you feeling today Mrs. Giordano?" asks Megan softly.

"Like shit," she says. "But don't tell the boys...or my Angelo over there."

Sitting in the corner of the room holding silent vigil is Angelo Giordano, her devoted, loving husband of sixty-two years. He looks frail and tired in his plain white button-down shirt and black slacks, his veined hands resting gently on a cane beneath his chin.

Angelo sits in this chair every day, grief stricken and silent, not knowing what to do or what to say to comfort his dying wife, refusing to leave her side ever since the hospital sent her home.

"My Angelo doesn't speak much English," says Mrs. Giordano. "In fact, all he ever says is 'I'm coming upstairs, Maria' and 'I'm finished, Maria.' Isn't that right, *mio bellissimo ragazzo.*"

She blows him a kiss. He sends one back as the sons begin to pop into the room one by one.

"Ma, you gotta taste this. Too much oregano, right?" asks Mario offering her a spoonful of gravy

Megan tries to intercept. "She really shouldn't..." But it's too late.

"Perfect baby," replies Mrs. Giordano gently removing the spoon from her lips.

Bruno rushes in. "Hey Ma, Silvio used the car last night and didn't fill the tank back up."

Silvio yells from the hallway, "I was in a hurry to get home to see my mother!"

Mrs. Giordano beams. "Such a good boy."

"It's on 'E' out there, Ma," complains Bruno. "Tell him to give me money for gas."

"I filled it last week!" Silvio barks now joining them in the bedroom.

Megan does her best to get control. "Guys, could you not...?" But it's no use. They continue to argue and pester their mother. It's just what they do.

"No, you didn't."

"The gravy, Ma. No good?"

"You like this shirt, right Ma?" asks Bruno pointing to the hideous blue silk.

"So handsome," Mrs. Giordano smiles at her son.

"It's mine!" shouts Stevie. "Tell him to take it off, Ma!"

The chubby brothers begin to struggle. It's all just posturing and head-bobbing, no punches are thrown. Ever. Megan has watched enough hockey games with her father to know when a real fight is about to erupt. She steps in to referee.

"Boys. Boys! Enough. Your mother needs rest and peace and quiet."

She looks to their father still sitting quietly in the corner, chin on his cane, unfazed by the ruckus.

"Mr. Giordano. Go. Go with your boys and eat. Mangia. Mangia," Megan says brushing them all out of the bedroom.

They all leave. Mrs. Giordano looks at Megan, impressed. "How come you're not married, a strong girl like you? What...you a lesbian?"

"I'm just waiting for my Prince Charming," Megan says, only half kidding.

"Go pick out one of my four boys. They'll make someone a nice husband."

"There's only four down there?" asks Megan. "Sounds more like forty."

"Marone," the old woman laughs in Italian slang. "The fighting. They keep it up they'll all end up alone...or even worse, together."

Megan smiles and begins to tuck the heavy blankets around Mrs. Giordano's bed. "Well, it's quiet now."

"They must be eating," says a resigned Mrs. Giordano. "That's what I miss the most. My kitchen. Dinners at the table. That's where we cook and we eat and we argue. The Italian soundtrack. It's the music of the house."

Megan smiles softly and repeats the words, "There should always be music. Would you like me to get you a radio?"

Mrs. Giordano waves a dismissive hand. "I'll just listen to the yelling. They should start up again around dessert." She looks Megan up and down. "You're too skinny. Go eat. I'll be fine."

"You sure?" asks Megan.

Mrs. Giordano lays her head deep into the pillow. "Yes. Sometimes it's good to be alone."

Megan thinks on that. Maybe she's right.

SOUTH BOSTON

Michael Evans gently taps on the back door of the Hayes house. He's pudgy and uncomfortable with his teenage awkwardness. Megan can tell from the softness of his knock that he's hoping no one will answer.

"Michael," she says opening the door. "Come in. You want some breakfast?"

He shakes his head 'no' and enters the kitchen as his dark brown eyes scan the room. He looks up to see rows of tacky shot glasses lined along the top of the cabinets. These are the 'presents' Jackie Boy would hurriedly grab at some gift shop before heading home. Each glass is from a different country and each one was opened and welcomed by his wife Polly as if they were treasured jewels from the Far East.

Suddenly, a loud noise comes from the basement.

"AAAAHGH!" THUD!

Michael jumps.

More noise from below. "AAAH!" THUD!
Michael's eyes widen.

"You sure?" asks Megan, unfazed by the noise. "I just made some eggs." Another loud scream comes from the basement. "AAAAAHH!" THUD!

Michael is frozen with fear. He stares at the basement door, afraid to move.

Another "AAAGH!" THUD!

"Go on down," Megan coaxes him. "He won't bite. I just fed him." She winks, trying to calm the terrified boy's fears.

The grunts and thuds grow louder as Michael descends the creaking wooden steps. He enters a basement that reeks of perspiration, turpentine and laundry detergent. The damp stone foundation walls are covered with Marine Corps banners and posters.

Michael stops on the bottom step and scans a makeshift room filled with old-school gym equipment, iron weight plates, and assorted paint cans filled with concrete. A military duffel bag stuffed with towels and hangs from the ceiling has 'US Navy' stenciled in white. (most Marines say it's a rivalry, but the truth is, Jackie Boy *hates* the Navy.) The leather weight belt, tire and chain lay neatly in the corner.

And then Michael finally spots Jackie Boy. He is standing against the stone foundation wall, sweat staining through his USMC T-shirt. His arms are extended, holding sand bags until, "AAAAGH!" he drops the bags to the floor. THUD!

"Who the hell are you?" growls Jackie Boy.

Michael steps back in fear. "I...I'm supposed to shovel your walk, because...because you can't?"

"Is that so?" shouts Jackie so Megan can hear him. "I can shovel my own Goddamn stoop!"

Megan yells back from the kitchen, "Stay away from that snow, LaLanne! I'm heading out. You need anything from the store?"

"Yeah," he shouts back. "Seventy row boats. And a mouth guard!" He turns his attention to Michael.

"I can shovel snow, ya know. Civilian doctors say the motion's no good for my lower back, or some Goddamn foolish thing. What's your name, kid?"

"Michael," the timid boy replies without moving a muscle. Jackie Boy eyes him up and down, clearly not impressed with what he sees.

"Let me guess. Capital M, small Y, capital K, a few E's and an L, right? My-Keele?" Jackie says doing his best to intimidate.

"No," replies the frightened boy. "It's just Michael."

"Uh, huh. Which Michael you named after, kid? Michael the basketball player or Michael the singer?"

"Michael the Archangel," he replies, growing confident.

Jackie Boy steps back and gives the kid the once over.

"Is that so. You take drugs?"

"No," snaps Michael.

"Sell 'em?"

"No," says Michael, his voice gaining even more confidence. "Not everyone that looks like me is a drug dealer."

Jackie appreciates the new-found confidence and replies, "Not everyone that looks like me is old and weak."

There's a long pause as the two eye each other up and down. Michael is the first to speak.

"What's all this stuff?"

"This is the original Planet Fitness, kid," replies Jackie Boy with great pride.

He points to the stairs.

"That's my StairMaster."

The paint cans of concrete.

"Dumbbells."

The leather weight belt, tire and chain.

"Elliptical."

The hanging duffel bag.

"My Squid sparring partner. And of course," he says, shaking his wrist. "I keep the old 'shake weights' in the bathroom with my girlie magazines."

Jackie laughs to himself, but Michael doesn't get the joke.

"You work out, kid?"

"Not really," Michael replies.

"Yeah. I didn't think so. Drop and gimme ten pushups," Jackie says as if he were commanding a new recruit.

"Huh?" Michael asks confused.

"Ten pushups," commands Jackie. "Now!"

Michael drops to the floor and attempts to push himself up. Jackie Boy kneels beside him, almost face to face.

"Do you even know who Michael the Archangel is? He is the Defender in Battle. He has the power of Almighty God himself. You got more Michael Jackson in you than Michael the Archangel, kid."

Michael quits after two attempts. Jackie stands up and grabs his worn copy of the Marine boot camp manual.

"Here. Study this," he says tossing it to Michael.

Michael awkwardly bobbles it in his hands and looks at the cover. "You...you used to be a Marine?"

"*I am a Marine*," barks Jackie Boy through gritted teeth.

"My dad was in the Army," responds Michael, unimpressed.

"Is that so," snaps Jackie Boy, equally unimpressed. "You know what it says on Page One of the Army Survival guide? 'Call the Marines'"

Michael has had just about enough. He places the manual down on Jackie's duct-taped bench press and turns to head back up the stairs.

"My mother said I had to shovel you out or she'd take my iPhone away. But, I didn't sign up for no boot camp."

"Stop right there, kid," commands Jackie Boy. But Michael keeps walking toward the stairs. Jackie bellows, "HALT!"

The boy freezes. Jackie Boy approaches and stands nose-to-nose. He speaks clearly, directly, with purpose and grit.

"Now you listen here *My-Keele*. Seventeen percent of children in this country are obese. You know what obese means? It's just a nice word for fat. Really, really fat. You know what I see in your future, kid? An obese, housebound diabetic who's gonna need the fire department to saw the door wider so they can haul your ass out! Do you want to be old, fat and blind son? Well, do you?!"

Michael is stung. And silent.

Jackie continues his rant. "I will *not* have some flabby, sugar sucking fat kid die on my watch shoveling snow off my front stoop. Do you read me loud and clear?" Jackie waits. "I said, do you hear me?!"

"Yes," replies Michael meek as a lamb.

"Yes, what?" commands Jackie.

"Yes, I hear you?" asks Michael, confused and afraid.

"Yes, *Sir*," snaps Jackie Boy. "Now. Say it like a man!"

"Yes, *Sir!*" says Michael with correct emphasis.

"That's better. We start basic training tomorrow. 0500." Jackie leans in close. "That means five in the morning, kid."

DUDLEY SQUARE – ROXBURY

The heavy rap beat of Jay-Z music booms out of car stereos and bounces off worn houses and brick apartment complexes in the tough Hispanic neighborhood of Dudley Square, an area of Boston besieged by high crime and poverty. Kids lean against a fenced basketball court of cracked asphalt. Sprayed graffiti covers the wall of nearby buildings. A drug dealing thug wearing a black do-rag scarf on his head stands on the corner and makes a shady transaction with one of his 'customers'.

Two men sit side-by-side in the oversized Chevy. Charlie Peters is fifty-four and heavy, with reddish, flushed cheeks. He hardly has any neck - it's as if his head seemed to grow out of his shoulders. His clothes are a rumpled, consignment store mess. He tells people his hair is thinning. It's not. Charlie is bald - a fact he refuses to accept because of the long mud flap combover he constantly struggles to keep in place.

Beside him, impeccably dressed, fifteen years his junior and a complete opposite is Jeremy Crowley. He is thin, a runner, a yoga enthusiast, an eater of all things healthy and a general complete pain in the ass.

"I used to play, you know," says overweight Charlie, looking toward the crumbled unused court.

"Rap music?" asks Jeremy.

"Basketball, smart ass."

Jeremy glances over at Charlie's stomach, the belt forming a deep gully. "You should really try to lose some weight, Charlie. I mean, even like ten pounds could really help."

"Yeah? Then what am I gonna do when I get there?" says Charlie, tugging at his tight belt. "I'd have to buy all new clothes. Get my teeth whitened. Buy a snazzy sports car. Leave my wife. Nah, way too much work. You skinny people are a real pain in the ass, you know that?"

Jeremy continues his amateur diagnosis. "What's your body mass index? I'm sure it's above normal range for your height and age."

"It's perfect," replies Charlie as he bites into a powdered donut just to piss him off.

"I'm sure it is," replies Jeremy with sarcasm. "If you were six foot five and eighteen years old."

"Just keep your eyes open and take the Goddamn pictures, smart ass," Charlie tells him, his lips covered with white sugar powder. "Here she comes."

Jeremy lifts his camera and aims it at the woman walking towards their car pushing a lightweight wheelchair filled with plastic grocery bags.

It's Megan Hayes.

****

Dudley Square is not the kind of place that takes notice strangers coming and going at all hours. It's the kind of neighborhood where people look away and don't get involved. Less trouble that way.

Megan walks up the housing development steps to the Lopez apartment. The hallway smells of weed, stale beer and urine. Empty beer bottles and trash accumulate in the corner.

Her spare key opens the door to the apartment and she enters a cluttered mess. Piles of laundry are littered atop worn furniture. There are no curtains or shades. Instead, blankets are nailed across the bare molding to cover the windows and wearied broken screens.

An elderly Hispanic man lays in a bed that has been moved to what is considered the Lopez family living room.

Beside the bed is Santiago Lopez, a hulking man-child, rocking rhythmically back and forth as he sits watching cartoons on the television across the room. Santiago has the heart of a ten-year-old and a mental capacity to match. A person his size could wreak havoc if he wanted to, but Santiago is a real gentle giant. At twenty-six years old he is out of school and out of the system, fallen between the cracks of a world that doesn't see him and doesn't seem to care.

Megan takes off her wool coat and looks at the sink filled with dirty dishes. A single fly buzzes incessantly over dried condiments and leftovers. Beside the faucet is a clear glass vase with a single red carnation standing inside. It's the signal (and the deal) Megan made with Santiago's father, Manny, letting her know that he came home - at least for a little while. Megan can't control Manny's bad luck or his bad booze, but she is trying her best to control his bad choices.

"Santiago, I told you I can get Social Services back in here to help," she tell him. "Would you like me to call them again?"

"No, Ma'am. I'm taking care of mi abuelito," says Santiago, his eyes finally leaving the television. He looks at the wheelchair. "How are you getting all these things, Miss Hayes? The insurance man said we didn't..."

"You let me worry about that, Santiago," says Megan as she begins unloading the groceries from the wheelchair into a bare fridge. "You just keep taking care of your grandfather. You're doing a very good job."

Megan walks to the window and pulls the back the blanket. "It's pretty cold out there," she says, squinting at the sunlight hitting the snow.

Santiago joins her at the window. "He likes to see the trees, Miss Hayes," says the devoted grandson. "He *needs* to see the trees."

They both look out at the cold morning, the tree branches are crusted in snow, bending deep beneath the heavy winter weight.

"Papi says 'Everyone loves something when it's healthy and blooming. When it's gray and sad and lonely... that's when it needs love the most.'"

Megan looks at her own face reflected in the glass. She seems gray and sad and lonely. "Your Grandfather is a very wise man," she says, then shakes her head and snaps out of it. "Now, let's you and I go over these pills first, OK?"

"Ok, Miss Hayes," smiles Santiago.

Megan removes a medicine bottle that was hidden inside her smock. Pills out onto an old wooden table cluttered with soda cans and empty Kraft macaroni and cheese boxes, remnants of the cheap, easy, unhealthy diet of a family living on the edge of the economy. She begins to distribute each pill into a 7-Day medication box.

"Now, he'll need *one* of these pills every *six* hours, and then *one* of these every day at *two* in the afternoon."

Santiago's face shows his confusion. "I'm, I'm not real good with my numbers and letters so much, Miss Hayes," he admits sadly.

Megan sighs, then turns to look at the cartoons playing on the television. Daffy Duck is trying to match wits with Bugs Bunny.

"Pronoun Trouble," she says aloud. "I love this one."

Santiago lights up. "You like Bugs Bunny? He's on every day at nine o'clock. Then SpongeBob at eleven. And Road Runner is on at two."

Megan gets an idea. She reaches for the stack of old VHS tapes that are piled beside the television. She slides the tapes from their cardboard sleeves and begins to rip the cartoon figures off each cover, then tapes the figures over the days of the week on the medication box. She draws numbers next to the characters, each symbolizing a dose.

"Here's what I want you to do, Santiago. When Bugs Bunny is on, you give your Grandfather this. SpongeBob, this one. Road Runner..."

"Si. Entiendo," says Santiago, grasping the idea. "This one. I got this, Miss Hayes. I got this."

Megan smiles wide. "I know you do. One thing at a time, OK? Let's get these numbers down, and then we'll work on your letters."

Santiago smiles confidently as they distribute the remaining pills. Megan makes a mental note to get to the dirty dishes in the sink, and discard today's red carnation for Manny.

But she'll get to all that later.

O'BRIEN FUNERAL HOME

If you're Irish, from Southie, and dead, then O'Brien's is the place to have your wake. The room smells of flowers, cheap perfume and whiskey breath unsuccessfully concealed by the free peppermints in the lobby.

Megan waits her turn in line, just like she's done so many times for so many patients over the years. She makes quick eye contact with a handsome man standing behind her and pulls her coat tight, trying to conceal the frumpy nursing scrubs she's still wearing from work.

'Act cool', Megan tells herself. 'You're in O'Brien's, not Murphy's.' People meet and fall in love every day. Why not at a wake on a Tuesday in February?

Out of the corner of her eye, Megan checks out the handsome man's left hand. Yep. There it is. A wedding ring. Oh well. So much for her great imaginary 'I can't believe you met your husband at a wake at O'Brien's?' story.

She thinks to herself, 'Why didn't I just stay home, eat a quart of Brigham's ice cream, watch the Bruins, and never get out of bed.'

Megan looks around the big room at the dark ornate furniture and her thoughts begin to drift to her mother. Polly

Hayes was from Southie. She was Irish. And, well, she had her service at O'Brien's.

Megan wonders if Jackie Boy will want to have his service here. 'Don't book anything,' her mother used to say. 'Your father thinks he'll live forever.' Megan smirks at memory.

When Polly Hayes was first diagnosed, Megan and her mother both agreed not to tell Jackie, afraid that the big tough Marine couldn't handle the news. But as the sickness spread, and she deteriorated quickly - quicker than Megan expected - Jackie started to notice little things with his wife. The loss of memory. Shortness of breath. Rapid weight loss. Eventually, the nurse in Megan had to tell him.

So, utilizing her best bedside training and all the professionalism she could muster, Megan told her father that his wife — and her mother - was dying.

Jackie refused to accept it, or even talk about it, thinking that if he ignored the illness it would somehow magically go away.

"You're gonna to need a battle plan," Polly said to Megan with a wink as she lay in bed, the cancer slowly tightening its grip.

Polly always knew how to comfort and make her daughter smile. Whenever Jackie Boy would get too 'military', barking his strict orders and setting unrealistic house rules, Polly would sit Megan on the edge of her bed and try to explain the complexities of her Drill Sergeant-like father. It was especially hard since Jackie and Megan were so similar in their stubbornness.

"Your father is a very complex man," Polly would tell a hurt and confused teenage Megan. "He believes in the institution over everything else. But you need to know he loves his family with all his heart and soul. He's a Marine, a husband, and a father. Sometimes the order gets mixed up, but he needs all three to survive."

As Megan got older, she came to accept her 'colorful character' of a father. But when her mother lay dying, she needed Jackie Boy to be more of a husband, and less of a Marine. Was that too much to ask? Megan would gladly take third position as daughter if he could just be there for Mom!

The wake's slow receiving line creeps forward and snaps Megan out of the memory. She kneels, says a quick prayer at the casket, then stands to express her condolences to the family. Maureen Farrell, the grieving widow, gives her a heartfelt hug.

"Oh, Megan dear, you were *so* good to my Billy."

Mrs. Farrell looks to the handsome gentleman standing in line behind Megan. "And you must be Joe. I've heard so much about you."

"Oh, no," says Megan, turning bright red. "This isn't...Joe and I...I'm so sorry."

Embarrassed, Megan hastily expresses her condolences to the rest of the Farrells, grabs a Mass card and rushes out.

MURPHY'S LAW, SOUTH BOSTON

Murphy's Law is a local Southie dive with an old school vibe, which means three things - strong drinks, gruff bartenders, and cash only. Black and white photos of Boston Irish politicians James Michael Curley, Ray Flynn and John F. Kennedy share the interior brick walls alongside sports legends Ted Williams, Larry Bird, and Bobby Orr.

Megan sits alone on a stool at the end of the bar. She hands the Mass card from O'Briens to the bartender, Tommy Driscoll. Tommy is a bit more affable to the locals. He has a mop of aging curly brown hair and a thick mustache that makes it appear that he doesn't have lips or a mouth.

73

He peers at the name through the thick glasses perched upon the tip of his pink nose, then drops the laminated Mass card into an oversized brandy glass snifter where it falls alongside several others.

"To William Farrell," says Tommy pouring whiskey into two shot glasses. "May he rest in peace."

Megan raises her glass and toasts in Gaelic.

"Slainte'."

They've done this routine before.

Megan scans the bar filled with couples, each locked in conversation and comfort. At the far end sits a man doing his absolute best *not* to look middle aged. His hair is a deep shade of chestnut with white roots peeking out from the scalp, reminding him that it's time to schedule that next hair color appointment. His complexion is professionally and *excessively* tanned, clearly the result of multiple visits to the tanning bed facility at his local strip mall. This guy makes George Hamilton look like Casper the Ghost.

He notices Megan sitting alone, then struggles to remove the wedding ring from his finger, slips it into his pocket, and starts to walk in her direction

"Can I buy you a drink, sweetheart?" he asks, dripping cockiness.

Megan mouths the words back to herself. 'Sweetheart?' He can't be serious.

"I'd really rather be alone," she replies, never turning around.

"Come on. One drink. Nobody wants to be alone," he says sliding into the empty barstool beside her. Megan is reminded of Mrs. Giordano's comment, 'It's good to be alone sometimes.' Especially now.

The tanned guy beckons Tommy. "Barkeep. Vodka rocks. What do you drink, sweetheart? Grey Goose? Absolut?"

Megan nods to the Tommy. "'Gansett." Tommy already has the bottle opened.

"Narragansett?" says her tanned bar-mate. "Might as well drink seltzer water. Wouldn't you rather have a fine IPA or a Dark Wheat beer? It's on me, Sugar."

'It's Sugar now? This guy can't be serious,' thinks Megan.

"Dark wheat is how I take my toast," she growls, her eyes never leaving the glass in front of her.

"So, Honey, what do you do when you're not drinking cheap beer?" he asks, trying to work his magic.

Megan rolls her eyes, 'Sweetheart? Sugar? Honey? What decade is this guy from?'

"I'm a hospice nurse," she replies hoping he'll just go away.

"Ooh, a 'Hot-Spice' nurse!" he says, dragging his bar stool closer. "I like that. Maybe I'll let you give me a nice sponge bath someday."

"Jesus," Megan mumbles. "What is the deal with you guys and the sponge baths?"

Now she's insulted and getting angrier by the second. Her right hand begins to clench. She's had just about enough. Then, slowly, her fist loosens, and her demeanor begins to change. She's got this.

"You know what?" she says, finally turning to face Tan-Man. "That sounds real good. Maybe I can take a warm sponge and wash it all over your body. Would you like that?"

Tanned guy is a bit taken aback at her sudden change, but readily accepts.

"Yeah. You bet."

"I'd start by washing your neck. Your back," she says as she leans closer and drags her hand to emphasize each movement. "Then your arms and ...wait, what's that? It's not washing off. Why, that's not dirt. It's a mole. That sure looks suspicious. All those days you spent lathering up on Revere Beach with Johnson's Baby Oil, trying to get the perfect tan to pick up the perfect girl. Well it's all coming back to bite you in the ass. That's not a mole at all. It's Melanoma. The doctors just told you, you have Stage 4 cancer. By the way, there's no Stage 5. Wow. What a gut punch, huh? You'll start chemo to stop the rapid progression of bad cells, but by then it's too late."

Tanned guy is confused. Megan continues her observations. "Your mornings will be spent throwing up as you watch clumps of your dyed black hair fall out. Radiation burns will take the place of that beautiful summertime glow of yours. And when you're a bald, withering, frail man who can't control his bladder? *That's* when this 'Hot-Spice' nurse will have to give you a sponge bath."

He's speechless - his tan replaced by ash white terror. Megan sips her beer and stares straight ahead.

"You want my advice, pal? Have the mole checked out or else I'll see you at O'Briens. Oh, and put the ring back on."

"Huh?" asks the reeling Casanova-wanna-be.

"The wedding ring," she says pointing to the white indent on his finger. "Goes right there along the *tan* line."

He stands to leave and mutters under his breath, "What a bitch."

Uh oh. Tommy's eyes widen. Chairs slide. A hush falls over the bar. Megan puts her beer down and turns to him.

"What did you just call me?"

But Tan-Man has scurried away. Megan tries to stand, but Tommy reaches over the bar and holds her back. "Settle down, Megan."

"Get me another, will ya, Tom?" she asks. Tommy frowns. It's awkward.

"What?" Megan asks.

"You still owe me from the other night."

"I'm good for it," she snaps.

Tommy knows she is, but Megan's credit is getting a bit extended. "I'll spot you for tonight, but that's it. Maybe you should stop buying wheelchairs." Megan knows what he means.

"Forget it," she says downing the last of her beer.

She places the empty bottle on the bar and heads out, mumbling under her breath, "bitch."

A few moments later, a new Murphy's customer pulls out the empty bar stool that Megan was in. He sits, unwittingly pushes her empty beer bottle aside and calls to Tommy.

"Gansett please."

Tim Wallace sits alone scanning the bar. He struggles to remove the wedding ring from his finger and slips it in his pocket.

WALLACE HOUSE - QUINCY, MA

Megan opens the bedroom curtains fluffing in the morning sun and begins her routine, once again picking up the framed photo of Mr. Wallace that was face down on the nightstand.

"Was he talking to you all night again?" Megan asks with a smirk.

Mrs. Wallace just smiles.

"Would you like another blanket, Mrs. Wallace? It's pretty cold."

Mrs. Wallace brushes off the suggestion.

"Oh, it's not that cold, Megan. I grew up in upstate New York. Troy. Winters there were bitter cold," she says as Megan begins to take her blood pressure. "My brother Dan used to deliver coal in the neighborhood. There was this one winter, oh it was so cold - his shoes had worn right through to his socks. I tied newspaper around his feet to help keep them warm. When he got home, the papers were frozen solid. Can you imagine?" She laughs softly at the memory. "We had to thaw his feet out by the fireplace, so I could get his boots off."

Megan smiles back, a hint of concern passing over her face from the blood pressure reading.

"So, no Megan, I'm not that cold. People today complain too much. You need to find the joy in every day," says Mrs. Wallace looking Megan in the eye and taking her by the hand. "You are my joy today. Thanks for listening to an old woman and her stories."

Megan smiles and replies softly, "I could listen to your stories all day."

Mrs. Wallace looks over Megan's shoulder. Tim has been standing quietly in the doorway, watching the tender scene before him. Megan is a bit embarrassed. She stands and fixes herself, unwittingly trying to make a better impression, then gestures Tim aside to speak privately.

"I'm concerned about your mother's blood pressure," she whispers. "I think her lungs may be getting filled with fluid. Those pillows aren't giving her enough support." She glances back to make sure Mrs. Wallace isn't listening. "I think it's time to get an electric bed."

Tim's face shows a reaction that says, 'I don't think she'll go for it.'

"You want me to talk to her?" asks Megan.

"You think you can sell it alone?" he replies.

Megan looks at him with her reassuring, cocky smirk. "I got this."

They approach Mrs. Wallace. Tim goes into sell mode first, his voice higher and happier.

"Hey Ma, how would you like a fancy new bed?"

"You mean a hospital bed, Timothy" replies Mrs. Wallace sharply.

"It's an electric bed, Mom," sells Tim as if he were trying to convince his daughter that broccoli tastes like French fries.

Megan speaks up to help. "It would elevate your head and increase oxygen flow."

"It's pretty sweet, actually," continues salesman Tim. "You would look really cool in it. Wouldn't she Megan?"

Megan catches his eye across the bed and she smirks at him. "Super cool."

Tim looks at Megan and smiles back, happy that she joined in the ruse. But Mrs. Wallace is having none of it. Her smile is gone. Her eyes lock on her son.

"Timothy. This is the bed I slept in with your father in for forty-six years. This is the bed you jumped into when you were frightened by thunderstorms. This is the bed you and I snuggled in and read 'Goodnight Moon.' This is *my* bed, Timothy. This is the only bed."

Her look says it all.

Tim looks to Megan and shrugs, defeated. "Well, I guess this is the bed."

Megan confirms the decision. "I'll get go more pillows."

Tim pivots to change the mood. "Ok, party people, it's Disco Night here at Studio Hayes. But first, our favorite part of the day. Medication time. What do you think, Ma? Shoe-shots or ice luge?"

Mrs. Wallace finally regains her smile. "Oooh, such a big decision. What do you think Megan?"

"I don't know," says Megan. "It's really not a good..."

But Tim interrupts before she can finish. "Definitely ice luge."

Mrs. Wallace agrees. "But we need music, Timothy. There should always be music."

****

Tim walks down the back steps and into the cold February morning to his black Ford Ranger Pickup parked in the driveway just below the basketball net his father hung off the garage decades ago. Megan follows him out.

"We have a protocol, Tim. If anything happens to your mother, she'll..."

"She'll what," he turns abruptly. "She'll get sick? Sicker?" His tone is a bit harsh, and he realizes it.

"Look, I realize this all seems a bit unorthodox. But these pretend Happy Hours, they're kinda my way of coping...and avoiding. I know she doesn't have much time left. I want it to be filled with good times and music."

The nurse in Megan knows this is all against the rules. It's a protocol disaster, and Tricia would certainly have her ass in a sling if she ever found out. But the daughter in Megan understands. She softens.

"My mother had two rules," she tells Tim. "Candles with every meal and music. There should always be music."

"She sounds like a fun lady," says Tim, relieved to have Megan's acceptance.

"She was."

"Oh, I'm so sorry," Tim says sincerely.

"It's OK. She was at home too. It's…it's good for people to spend their final days surrounded by loved ones and memories, instead of medicine bottles and electric hospital beds," says Megan, trying to deflect the hurt.

Happy with his victory, Tim hops onto the bed of the truck and maneuvers a bicycle that's been strapped to the back. "I do a ten-mile loop in the mornings from my place in the city through Castle Island and back. The other day, I see this old man jogging with a chain wrapped around his waist and he's pulling a tire. Guy must be 70 years old."

"Actually he's 68," mumbles Megan loud enough for Tim to hear.

"You've seen him?"

"Every morning," she replies flatly.

"Quite a colorful character, huh?"

"You have no idea," Megan whispers under her breath.

Tim pushes the bike aside to get to an oversized cooler.

"You ride?" he asks. Megan shakes her head. "Me? No. Not really. I never learned how."

Tim stops in astonishment. "What? Didn't your father ever teach you to ride a bike?"

"My father wasn't around much. He was…I mean he *is* a Marine. He taught me important things like how to spit polish shoes, make my bed so you can bounce a quarter on it, and disable an enemy combatant."

Tim does an exaggerated hand chop in the air. "Cool. Special Forces judo move?"

"Kick him in the nuts," deadpans Megan with a smirk.

Tim laughs hard. "All my father ever taught me was how to pour him a scotch. Two fingers. These two," he says opening a wide space between his pinky and index finger. "Not these two," his index and middle fingers are tight together.

Tim hops off and folds down the rear bed of truck. That daily bike loop has certainly helped carve a tight athletic frame. 'And good God,' Megan thinks to herself, 'why does he have to have such a nice butt?!'

She quickly diverts her eyes when he turns.

"The first scotch usually chilled him out," says Tim sliding the cooler. "Then he'd just get moody and angry."

Megan speaks up to help. "Well, I'm sure he'd be very proud of you."

"I doubt it. Nothing I did was ever good enough. Even pouring a simple drink. That man was really tough to satisfy."

"So, I heard," says Megan spitting a laugh remembering Mrs. Wallace's 'the man was insatiable' comment. The joke is lost on Tim.

"But my father *did* teach me how to give a proper salute," Megan says with pride. She stands at attention and starts to imitate Jackie Boy.

"Raise your right hand until the tip of your forefinger touches your right eye. Thumb and fingers extended. Hand and wrist straight. Forearm inclined at forty-five degrees. Then, drop your hand smartly to your side."

Tim attempts a salute. It's awful. Megan stifles a laugh. "We'll have to work on that."

"I'll tell you what. You teach me to salute, I'll teach you to ride a bike. Deal?"

"Deal."

They shake hands and smile as the cold relationship of the 'Fun-Police' nurse and the 'Immature Patient's Son' finally beginning to thaw. Their hands stay locked together for a few seconds longer than they should.

"Well," says Tim, finally braking the daze. "It's Disco time!"

With that, Tim reaches into the front seat of the truck to retrieve a powder blue tuxedo jacket and an oversized colorful Afro wig. He throws on the outfit and gives an exaggerated John Travolta 'Saturday Night Fever' hip check and finger point.

Megan watches as 'Disco Tim' rolls the cooler of ice towards the house, and whispers to herself, "Yup, quite a colorful character."

HOSPICE CENTER

Dr. Stanley Powers swivels his chair around and peers beyond the plastic anatomically-correct model heart on his desk to Tricia.

"I wanted to congratulate you on your promotion, Patricia. We all felt you would make a worthy Team Leader for our hospice staff."

"Thank you," says Tricia proudly. "I'm honored you considered me."

The truth is, Patricia wasn't the Board's first choice. She's cold and distant and not friendly with the staff, but they didn't have a much of a choice when their top candidate turned the offer down. As CEO, Dr. Powers knows Patricia is meticulous with detail and would alleviate any headaches that he might have to deal with, so it might as well be her.

"I'm sure your patients miss you," he continues trying to be cordial. Tricia leans forward.

"Really? Which ones? Did any of them ask for me?" she quickly replies, then suddenly realizes by the confused look on Dr. Powers face that he made the comment more as a courtesy than based on any fact. She immediately loses her enthusiasm.

"Of course. You wouldn't know that. How would you know that? I... I do miss the bedside nursing. Someone to talk to. Someone to listen. But, well my husband Edward thought this new job would be good for my career. The increase in pay. The 401K match. But, it's all very good and fine," she says, her voice trailing off as she looks to her lap.

Dr. Powers gets back to business. "Yes. Well, I imagine so. I'd like to discuss this year's Compassion Award with you."

"Of course," says Tricia regaining her composer.

"As you know," he continues, "it's our highest honor and goes to the employee who most exemplifies our values. Compassion. Integrity. Leadership. Respect."

Tricia smiles wide, thinking to herself, 'a promotion *and* an award. This *is* a good day.'

Dr. Powers continues. "Someone the staff looks up to and loves." Tricia's smile fades.

"This year it was unanimous," he continues. Her shoulder's slump.

"Megan Hayes," he says with smiling eyes. "We thought it would be appropriate for you to present the award, since you are the new Team Leader."

Ouch. Tricia is privately seething.

"Yes, certainly," she replies in the most professional tone she can muster.

Dr. Powers removes his glasses and leans forward in his chair, his pleasant, professional tone is gone, replaced with sternness. "Now, this business about the dispensary. You need to get this under control, Patricia. You're in charge now."

Tricia nods her head, "I understand."

"Besides a public relations nightmare, this is an economic loss, a violation of countless regulations, and a potential lawsuit. So, what are you doing about it?"

Tricia sits up, all stoic and starchy, then imitating Megan's cocky smirk, she says with voice of pure venom, "I got this."

MRS. WALLACE ROOM - QUINCY, MA

"Karaoke time!" sings 'Disco Tim' dressed his powder blue tuxedo and Afro wig. "What do you want me to play, Ma?"

Mrs. Wallace is giddy with anticipation. "You know what I want to hear, Timothy."

He does, and plugs the selection into his karaoke boom box. Tom Jones begins to sing.

It's not unusual to be loved by anyone
It's not unusual to have fun with anyone

Tim begins to do his best Tom Jones impersonation - and it's honestly not that bad! Swirling jacket. Gyrating hips. Swinging microphone. He looks ridiculous - and his mother loves it.

Megan laughs to herself as she helps Mrs. Wallace into a wheelchair and they roll her to the base of the ice-luge. Cherry Red Gatorade and medications are poured through a narrow channel carved in the block.

"Any way we can get it in," says Mrs. Wallace with the coy smile of guilty pleasure. Megan can't help but laugh.

But when I see you hanging about with anyone

It's not unusual to see me cry

Tim keeps dancing and singing like Tom Jones, taking his mother's hands and gently swaying her to the music. Suddenly, a pair of over-sized Granny-pants underwear land on Tim's head. They both turn to Megan's direction. She shrugs innocently but looks guilty-as-sin standing beside an open dresser drawer. They all crack up laughing.

Tim approaches Megan and gently holds her by the waist. She waves him off at first, but he persists, and the look on Mrs. Wallace's face tells Megan to go on, dance with her son. Tim and Megan begin to dance and smile and laugh, twirling around the room.

He dips Megan deep from the waist as they lean into the music. Their eyes meet and hold a moment. And a moment more, his hand lightly holding the small of her back. The music plays on. Everything is perfect, as if they were the only two people in the room, the only two people in Boston, the only people on Earth.

A cough is heard. Small at first, then uncontrollable. Their trance is broken. Tim and Megan turn to see a spittle of blood on Mrs. Wallace's lip. Megan instinctively rushes to her side, the nurse in her reacting fast as lightning. She looks back to Tim, trying to control the panic in her voice. "Get me some towels."

Mrs. Wallace looks at Megan, terrified and confused. "Dan? Where is Dan? He'll be cold. I...I need to start the fire."

She tries to stand, her face desperate, searching. Megan holds her by the shoulder.

"I'll get his boots off. Don't worry. Dan's going to be alright," Megan says in a calm reassuring manner.

Mrs. Wallace's eyes dart around the room. She looks lost. "Megan? Megan, I'm scared."

"I'm right here," she tells the frightened, frail woman. "I'm right here beside you," and gently lays Mrs. Wallace back down in her bed.

"I'm so happy Timothy found you," whispers the frail woman as her head sinks into the pillows. "I was afraid he was going to be alone." Megan doesn't know how to respond.

"You're a good daughter," whispers Mrs. Wallace.

Megan goes with it. "And you're a great mother."

Tim stands alone in the doorway holding towels, breathless, terrified and confused, as he watches Megan caress his mother's forehead.

HAYES HOUSE - SOUTH BOSTON

Michael stands against the stone basement wall, his arms extended, attempting to hold bags of sand that are only a quarter filled.

"Come on," Jackie Boy barks at him. "You've got more in you than that!"

"My hands are still frozen from shoveling your steps this morning," says Michael with a thud, dropping the bags to the floor.

"Never make excuses. Ever," Jackie Boy barks. "And it's not that cold. You kids today complain too much. You think your father complained like this when he was in the Army?"

"I don't know," Michael replies, the mention of his father clearly a sore subject. "My dad never talked much about the Army. He just yelled a lot. At my mom. At me mostly. Said I was fat and lazy." Michael looks to his feet and shrugs his shoulders. "I think that's why he left."

An uncomfortable silence hangs over them. Jackie looks at the sad, lonely boy. "Goddamn Army grunt leaving his post in the middle of a mission. Well, you're in my unit now. And a good Marine never leaves a man behind. How old are you, kid?"

"Almost seventeen," Michael replies.

Jackie smirks. "I was about your age when I decided to join the Corps. Didn't even lick the frosting off my birthday candles and I was down at the enlistment office lying about my age. Most kids from my neighborhood went into the service because they dropped out of school, or so they wouldn't go to jail. Not me. I always wanted to be a Marine."

Michael is now genuinely intrigued. "Was it really tough?"

"Not as tough as I'll be on you if you don't give me one more set!" Jackie barks.

Michael grabs for his sweatshirt pocket. "I need to get some pump-up music," and begins typing on his iPhone. The hard beat of Rap music begins to play from the small speaker. Jackie Boy's face scrunches in pain. "What the hell is that noise?"

"That's Jay-Z," beams Michael, his head bopping to the music.

"Jay *who?*" asks Jackie, clearly displeased.

"Come on, man, everyone knows Jay-Z! He's a rapper. Producer. He's got fourteen Grammys. And to top it off, he's married to my dream girl, Beyonce."

Jackie Boy is lost. "Kid, I have absolutely no idea what you're talking about."

Michael begins to rap along with the music.

99 Problems but a bitch ain't one.

If you havin' girl problems I feel bad for you son.

I got 99 problems but a bitch ain't one.

Jackie Boy jumps as if he were electrocuted and scoots over to the basement stairs in horror.

"Are you crazy? Using the B word?! What if Megan heard you?" he says looking up the stairwell like a frightened child. "She may look all sweet and nurse-like, but that little girl of mine is Southie-tough...God love her."

He looks up the stairs to confirm the coast is clear, and asks, "Do girls today really put up with this stuff?"

"What stuff?" asks Michael.

"Calling them…you know, the *B-word,*" utters Jackie Boy, making sure the last part was a whisper.

"Some do, I guess," replies Michael. Jackie Boy regains his Marine Corps demeanor. "Well shame on them. You need to respect women, you copy?"

"Yes," says Michael.

Jackie scowls and waits for it.

"I mean, Sir. Yes, sir."

"That's better," says Jackie Boy and heads over to a corner of the basement. "I'll show you some real music."

With dramatic flourish he peels back a white cloth to reveal an old Wurlitzer Jukebox. Michael's eyes go wide as saucers. He's never seen anything like this. He reaches for the stack of old 45's piled on the floor.

"Careful there, Mister," commands Jackie Boy in the same tone he reprimanded Megan. Michael looks at the plastic record in his hand with curiosity and wonder. "How many songs does it play?"

"One...well two, if you, um, if you flip it over," says Jackie as if suddenly realizing how ridiculous that sounds.

Michael holds up his iPhone. "This plays two hundred songs."

"Yeah, two hundred bad ones," Jackie replies quickly.

Lights illuminate the old Jukebox to life as Jackie Boy pushes the plastic buttons to select a song. Inside, mechanical arms rotate, and belts swing to place a 45 onto the turntable. Pops and scratches come through the speakers, then give way to a bouncy beat. Jackie's face lights up. He closes his eyes, lost in the moment as Bobby Darin begins to croon.

> *Oh, the shark, babe, has such teeth, dear*
> *And he shows them pearly white*
> *Just a jackknife has old MacHeath, babe*
> *And he keeps it, ah, out of sigh*

"Now, this is music, kid," yells Jackie over the music, snapping fingers along to the rhythm.

> *Ya know when that shark bites with his teeth, babe*
> *Scarlet billows start to spread*
>
> *start to spread...start to spread...start to spread*

Jackie's trance is broken. The record is skipping.

"What's wrong?" asks Michael.

"Aw, Goddamn it," growls Jackie Boy. He tries to remedy the situation by banging on the side of the Jukebox. But it's no use. The record's a goner.

"I can't believe you don't know what rap is, old man," says Michael.

"I know what rap is, kid," Jackie snaps. "The Marines invented it. Only, we call it Cadence."

"Cadence?" asks Michael. "What's Cadence?"

A sinister grin forms across Jackie Boy's face. He has an idea.

CASTLE ISLAND PARK

Jackie Boy and Michael are jogging side by side along the asphalt sidewalks of Southie. Jackie Boy begins to sing in cadence.

You can keep your Army khaki

You can keep your Navy blue

I have the world's best fighting man to introduce to you

His uniform is different

the best you've ever seen

The Germans called him Devil Dog

His real name is Marine.

He prompts a call-and-response from Michael. "Repeat after me, kid. *Momma, momma, don't you cry.*"

"*Momma, momma, don't you cry,*" puffs Michael, breathing hard.

"*Marine Corps motto is Semper Fi.*"

"*Marine Corps motto is Semper Fi.*"

A sly, mischievous smirk forms on Jackie's face. He alters the next line.

*"I got 99 Problems but **jock itch** ain't one."*

'That's funny,' thinks Michael, smiling. It's the wide, pleasant smile of a boy finally having fun, and one that Jackie has never seen on Michael's face. And that makes him smile too. Michael laughs and tosses a verse back.

*"If you havin' **crotch** problems I feel bad for you son."*

Jackie replies, "*I got 99 problems, **jock itch** ain't one. Oorah!*'

Leaning against a fence off in the distance is the teenage punk from the bus incident. His eyes narrow with anger as he watches the old man and the chubby boy slowly jog along the edge of Boston Harbor.

****

On the other side of the park, Tim is preparing to help Megan learn how to ride a bike. She's wearing knee pads, wrist pads, elbow pads, and a catcher's chest protector. Basically, wherever there is Megan, there is padding. She looks ridiculous - and terrified. Tim tries not to laugh.

"Your 'pad-to-person' ratio is pretty high there."

"I plan on falling. A lot," she says tugging at the 'wedgie' stuck in her sweatpants. Suddenly, pack of Spandex-clad cyclists speed by. Tim yanks her back, instinctively pulling her out harm's way.

"That was close," he says, glaring as the bikes roll by. "I don't get the outfits. It's just riding a bike. Sweatpants and a T-shirt work just fine."

Megan eye's squint. She's beginning to notice how much Tim sounds like her father.

"Ok, you ready?" asks Tim full of salesy enthusiasm as he steadies the bike. Megan takes a deep breath and gets mentally prepared to shove off.

"You sure you have time for this?" she asks, kind of hoping he doesn't. "I mean, I don't want to take you away from your family."

"Huh? No. No. They're busy with activities," says Tim as if he's said that a hundred times before, then gives the bike a push. "Now, go. Go!"

Megan pedals, slowly, wobbly. Tim jogs beside her, resembling Michael and Jackie Boy jogging on the opposite side of the park. Megan begins to pedal faster. Tim is huffing and puffing, trying to keep up. She smirks and accelerates, almost teasing him. Her eyes go wide. She's doing it! Megan Hayes is riding a bike!

"I got this!" she yells happily. "I got this!"

Tim stops to catch his breath and watches her with a carefree, proud grin. Megan is having a blast. She circles back past Tim. He playfully stands at attention, shoulders back, arms straight, and snaps her a smart salute. She laughs with glee.

There's a slight decline in the road, then a sharp turn. Tim's smile disappears.

"Oh, shit."

He runs, but it's too late. *BAM!* Amateur cyclist Megan Hayes is now on the cold ground, the wheels of her bike spinning in the air. Tim rushes to her side.

"Did you see me?" shouts Megan, elated. "I was riding a bike!"

"I did," Tim replies making sure she's OK. "Next time we'll work on stopping."

Tim takes her by the hand and pulls her up. Megan smiles wide, her hand still in his as they stand facing each other. Their eyes meet. No words are spoken, just chests heaving as the two of them catch their breath.

But something is wrong. Megan looks down at Tim's hand in hers. She snaps back to reality when she feels the cold hard metal on his ring finger.

"Megan, I..." he starts, but Megan's eyes are looking over his shoulder. Shit! Jackie Boy and Michael are jogging in their direction.

"I'm so sorry. I...I gotta go," she says then turns and runs away, mixing into the anonymous everyday crowd.

"Megan, wait!" he pleads. But she's gone.

Tim stands alone, twisting the gold wedding ring round and round on his finger.

Jackie Boy and Michael jog on by.

BEACON HILL

Tim Wallace enters a darkened room and turns on the light revealing an impressive, architecturally stunning apartment with gleaming hardwood floors. The large French windows overlook glistening, icy trees along Boston's Public Gardens.

He walks through the empty apartment and clicks another switch that illuminates a room filled with dolls and toys. A tiny easel is covered in children's drawings.

He turns the off light. After a moment of staring into the darkness, he decides to turn the lights back on.

A three-day pile of mail lays on the floor below the brass mail slot in the heavy mahogany door. Phone bill. Light bill. A notice from the Boston Public Library. A slew of ads and women's apparel catalogues. Tim tosses them all in the trash, along with a couple of handwritten Hallmark cards addressed to Tim Wallace.

He enters the sleek modern kitchen with brushed silver appliances and presses a button on the answering machine beside the phone.

"Hi, Hon. You're probably still at the office. We'll just meet you there later. OK?"

"Love you Dad!"

Tim looks at his watch. It's late. Again. He opens the fridge and checks the expiration date the milk carton - passable - takes a swig and leans against the counter, surveying the room just as stray cat appears at the window.

"You again, huh?"

Tim pours the last of the milk into a bowl and joins the cat out on the fire escape.

SOUTH BOSTON

The Hayes kitchen is covered with Island Luau decorations.

Plastic palm trees. Tiki torches. Strands of fake hibiscus. Megan leans against the counter wearing a grass hula skirt and Hawaiian shirt as Jackie Boys enters through the back door.

"What the hell is all this?" he asks with a scowl.

"Happy Hour," Megan replies in an overly cheerful tone.

"Happy *Hour*?" growls Jackie. "You mean I gotta put up with this for sixty minutes?"

Megan drapes a purple lei around her unhappy father's neck and hands him a rum-filled pineapple overflowing with colorful fruits and umbrellas.

"Here," she says. "Jimmy Buffett and boat drinks."

"I'm more of a Dean Martin and scotch kinda guy," Jackie grumbles.

"Come on, Dad! It'll be fun!"

"Now you wanna have fun? What the hell's gotten into you lately?" he asks.

"What do you mean?" replies Megan, enjoying her new-found giddiness.

"You got fifty-eight minutes," snaps Jackie Boy and sucks deeply on the neon green straw in his pineapple cocktail. Megan plops a straw hat on his head and with a really bad Jamaican accent says, "Come on, Mon. Relax and enjoy with I."

Jackie takes another long sip on the straw and looks at his watch.

"Fifty-six minutes."

Megan's shoulders stiffen. "Sure. But you have all the time in the world for Michael."

"What's that supposed to mean?" he asks, baffled.

"Nothing," she says brushing at her grass skirt, thinking maybe this was a bad idea. "I know you always wanted a son." Jackie is clearly hurt by the accusation. "I never said that."

"You never had to," she replies more matter of fact than with any deep seeded resentment. "You know you never even taught me how to ride a bike?"

"Jesus, here we go again," says Jackie Boy with an eye roll. "'I'm a terrible father. I was never around.' Well, sorry, kiddo. I was a little busy protecting the world and making it safe for democracy." And he means it.

He takes another long sip from the pineapple. "Besides, I tried to teach you to ride a bike when you were six. You crashed once and were too afraid to get back on."

Megan pauses for a moment, thinking about how much fun she had with Tim Wallace today - and she feels guilty. "Well, Loretta appreciates all the time you're spending with Michael."

Jackie Boy puffs his chest as the rum starts to take effect. "Kid's probably never seen so much toughness and virility before."

Megan looks at him. Tilted straw hat on his head. Purple flower lei around his neck. Sipping rum from a pineapple.

"Yep, I'm sure he never has," she quips.

The back-door swings open and Davey bounces into the kitchen. He looks around the room, amazed by the decor.

"I love it," he exclaims. "Island theme?"

"Happy hour," replies Megan.

"Forty-two minutes," snaps Jackie Boy holding up his pineapple at Megan. "Hit me again."

He looks at Davey. "Don't you ever knock? Just because you rent upstairs, that doesn't give you permission to come and go as you please."

Davey grabs Jackie's straw hat and rubs the white stubble of his crew cut. "Oh, you know you love me, Jackie Boy." Then puts the hat back and adjusts it with a proper tilt. He always knows how to tweak the gruff Marine.

Davey joins Megan by the sink to mix more rum, and whispers covertly, "Did you ask him yet?"

"I was gonna wait till he was on his third pineapple," she says out the side of her mouth. They both look at Jackie Boy. Straw hat. Lei around his neck. Scowl on his face.

"Here," she says to Davey handing him the bottle of Gosling's. "Add more rum. Like, a lot. I'll go help set the mood."

With that, Megan sneaks off to the living room and slides an album from Jackie's prized collection as Davey empties the bottle Gosling's Black Seal into the pineapple. She carefully, *gingerly* drops the needle on the spinning record.

Don Ho begins to sing.

Tiny bubbles

In the wine

Make me happy

Make me feel fine

Slowly, Jackie Boy's gruff scowl fades. The old saying is true - 'Music does sooth the savage beast.' Megan looks at Davey as if to say, 'OK, it's game time.'

"Dad," she says in her most conniving, slick tone. But she chickens out. "Davey wants to ask you something"

"Ask me what?" says Jackie. The booze and Don Ho's Tiny Bubbles beginning to unguard him.

"Well," begins Davey timidly. "I was just wondering...." He looks to Megan. She urges him to keep asking.

"Kevin and I are going to 'An Officer and a Gentleman' party this weekend. And.....can I borrow your uniform?" Davey shrugs his shoulders and looks at Megan with a defeated question mark on his face.

"Touch that uniform and you'll be pulling bamboo out of your fingernails," barks Jackie. "And I'll have you both know that uniform still fits," he adds proudly rapping at his waist.

Megan looks to Davey. This is our chance. They begin to scheme.

"There's no way," she says with fake enthusiasm.

"I don't think he can," replies Davey joining in on the con.

"Oh yeah?" replies Jackie. "I'll prove it to you."

He stands, a bit tipsy and off balance, and heads to his bedroom.

Davey joins Megan at the table, both pleased with their plan in action, and gives her an easy high-five.

"Yahtzee!"

"So, you gettin' excited for the big day?" she asks.

"I am," he replies, beaming. "I found that special someone, ya know? Someone to have coffee with in the morning, and wine with at night. And everything in between. It's perfect."

"I'm happy for you, Davey. I really am."

He looks around at the Hawaiian decor. "I like this 'Hawaiian Happy Hour Megan.' You're almost fun again."

"What do you mean, almost?" she asks, a bit offended. "I'm fun."

He gives her a long, knowing look. "Megan. We've been best friends since, what, eighth grade?"

"Seventh," she corrects him. "We were at the bus stop and Jimmy Burke called you a fag. I wouldda' beat the snot out of him too, if Jackie Boy didn't come runnin'."

"Jimmy's just lucky he didn't call you a bitch," laughs Davey.

"Yahtzee that, brother," she replies, and they slap five again.

Davey turns serious. "It's been a long time since you've been fun, Megan. You think it's a coincidence every relationship you have ends in death? Or just ends? You're afraid to fall in love again."

The words hit her right between the eyes. He realizes that, and softens his delivery. "There's someone out there for you, Megan. And it certainly wasn't 'Mass-hole' Joe."

"You mean, like, I just need to get back up on that bike?" she asks sarcastically.

"What?" Davey is confused.

"Forget it. It's a metaphor," she replies flatly.

Davey looks at her with a tilt of his head. They've been friends a long time. He can get away with saying things that other people can't say - or are afraid to say.

"You're a great hospice nurse, Megan. It protects you from the living."

The words hit Megan hard. Davey's right.

"I just, I want it on my terms, ya know?" Megan admits. "Not Joe's. Not Tricia's. Certainly not Jackie Boy's. Mine." Davey takes her hand and the two friends sit in silence.

"See! Told you!" yells Jackie Boy as he re-enters the room, beaming with pride in his Marine Dress Blues.

. His lean body still looks good in uniform - except for the straw hat tilted atop his head.

"You should really wear that out more," says Davey with dripping sarcasm.

"Ya think?" asks Jackie, seriously wondering.

"Absolutely," agrees Megan.

"Maybe you're right." Jackie buys it. Davey looks at Megan. Megan looks at Davey. Now's their chance.

"Dad," she says cheerfully, almost singing. "We have a little favor to ask you."

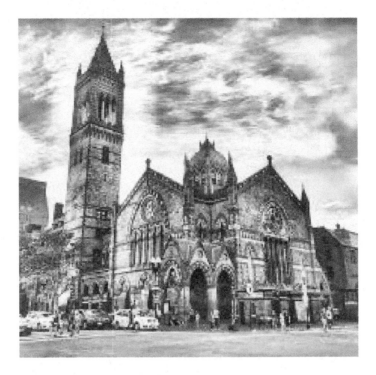

OLD SOUTH CHURCH

When Massachusetts was one of the first states to allow marriage for same sex couples, there was an immediate rush among the gay community to book churches that would allow such ceremonies. Boston's historic Old South Church embraced the Christian LGBTQ community. Carved into the stone of the church portico is the verse from Revelation 3:8 that reads *"Behold, I have set before you an open door, and no one can shut it."*

At the grand, gothic entrance of the church stands Jackie Boy Hayes, dressed sharp in his Marine Dress Blues. He has a pained scowl on his face, as if he's in agony. Beside him, absolutely beaming, stands Davey.

Megan approaches the unlikely couple. She looks at Davey, suave, sophisticated, and impeccably styled in a designer tuxedo, and laughs to herself, picturing Tim Wallace in his ridiculous powder blue tuxedo and Disco Afro wig. She turns to her father.

"Don't say a word," growls Jackie Boy. "Not one word."

"You look very handsome, Dad," says Megan fixing the brim of his white military cap.

"Told you it still fits," says Jackie, proudly tugging at his uniform. Megan kisses her father on the cheek and heads off to find a seat among the rows of ornate hand-carved wooden pews.

"I thought it'd be her I'd be walking down the aisle," Jackie says with a hint of sorrow, watching her walk away.

Davey nods. "Yeah, well...I thought it would be my own father but...he's too ashamed to be here," he says echoing Jackie's sadness and stare. "You'd like him, though. He was in the Navy."

"Navy man, huh?" growls Jackie hearing the hurt in Davey's voice. "Goddamn Squids, always expecting a Marine to get the job done for them. Well, the Marines are here now. Like always."

Davey smiles warmly and takes Jackie's arm. "You always were, Jackie Boy. I thought you were gonna break Jimmy Burke's arm that day." Jackie snorts a laugh at the memory. "Burkie. Dinky little runt. It was just a little twist of his wrist. He needed to be taught some manners, is all. What ever happened to that kid?"

"He went into politics. Worked for Barney Frank," says Davey.

"The gay Congressman?"

"Karma's a bitch, huh?" laughs Davey.

"Yahtzee that brother," smirks Jackie Boy.

They both stare down at the long aisle before them.

He turns to Davey and straightens his tie, firmly and perfectly, the way a father teaches a son. "Alright. Let's get this show on the road."

Organ music bounces off the carved Italian cherry woodwork, limestone, and stained glass as Jackie begins his slow walk down the aisle with Davey by his side.

Michael Evans is sitting alongside his mother Loretta. He smiles and gives Jackie Boy a big thumbs up as they approach. Jackie's eyes shoot daggers and drill him with a look, prompting Michael to jump in his seat and turn stone-faced toward the pulpit.

Jackie Boy continues his own slow death march, until finally, mercifully, he makes it to the alter and hands Davey off to his husband-to-be, Kevin.

Mission accomplished.

RECEPTION HALL

Jackie Boy sits at his assigned table, the stubble of his military crewcut and Marine uniform contrasting sharply to the room full of flamboyant guests in brightly colored outfits, man-buns and well-coiffed facial hair. A smug-looking waiter slides a plate of food in front of him. It's a tiny lamb chop garnished with baby carrots on a small bed of couscous.

"Christ almighty," Jackie growls to himself. "Even the food is gay."

He stands and taps a fork against his tumbler of scotch.

"I'd like to make a toast," he booms, comfortable in his sense of command. Megan scans the room and thinks to herself, 'Oh boy, this oughta be good.'

"For those of you unfortunate enough not to know who I am, my name is Captain John Donald 'Jackie Boy' Hayes. United States Marine Corps."

"My best man," shouts Davey. "Yahtzee!" The guests all laugh.

"Best man is right," continues Jackie Boy. "I am a Marine. A member of the proudest, most elite group of fighting men in the history of the world. I had the privilege to serve with men of courage. Men who know what it feels like to be outnumbered and still stand your ground."

His eyes are fixed on Davey and Kevin.

"It takes a special breed to stand for what you believe in, especially when the odds are against you."

They get it, and so does everyone else in the room, all listening intently.

"I was taught to size up situations and react. Lives depended on my decisions and judgements. And sometimes, well, sometimes those judgements can be wrong. You can be wrong about strength. You can be wrong about commitment."

This time his eyes are on Michael.

"You can be wrong about people."

Loretta smiles and takes her son by the hand. Jackie Boy continues.

"You need to learn to adapt. Learn to change. And you learn to never give up, because you know there are men, better men, who will be on the way."

Now he is looking directly at his daughter, speaking to Megan as if she's the only person in the room.

"You just need to be patient. And never settle. You deserve that. You deserve the best."

Megan quickly wipes away a tear hoping no one will notice.

"That takes courage," continues Jackie Boy, his voice rising as if giving an order. "And when you're that courageous, you will have the respect of the people around you. Today, you have my respect."

He raises his glass high. "To David and Kevin. And to Corps and Country. Oorah!"

The crowd cheers in unison, "Oorah!"

****

Soft music plays as Megan and Jackie Boy slow dance on the gleaming hardwood floor, her arms wrapped around her father's neck.

"You did a good thing today Dad. I'm proud of you."

"You know me," Jackie grins. "All sunshine and lollipops."

He glances around the dance floor at the other couples, a veritable potpourri of men with men, women with women, all slow dancing together. "So, when am I gonna walk *you* down the aisle?" he asks.

Megan gives a resigned sigh and looks off. "Marriage is overrated. Besides, fifty-percent of them end in divorce."

"There you go again," Jackie scolds. "You're never gonna to find someone with that gloomy attitude of yours."

She lays her head on his shoulder and thinks. 'He's right. And maybe Tim Wallace and Davey are right too. God, I *am* the 'Fun Police.' Her eyes find Michael sitting alone at his table, playfully trying on Jackie's white military cap.

"At least *you* found someone," she sighs.

"Michael?" replies Jackie. "He's a good kid. Just needs discipline. Positive role models. Hard work and regimented training..."

Megan stops dancing and looks at her father. "You didn't..."

After a moment Jackie pleads, "It was his idea not mine!"

"Wait, so, are you gonna tell Loretta he wants to join the Marines?"

Jackie stands before of his daughter and addresses her directly, succinctly, and with purpose.

"Megan, I've been shot at in Korea and Vietnam. I've studied the battle techniques of Communists, rebel insurgents and Russian equipped Cubans. Fought just about every mean S.OB. around the globe. But I'll tell you something. There is *nothing* deadlier, nothing more powerful or terrifying in this world than an angry black woman."

He pleads with his daughter, "Can you tell Loretta? Pretty please?"

****

At the reception's cocktail bar, Tricia and her husband Edward Coughlan are at it again. Arguing like hell. No one can tell what's being said, but it's clear that Tricia is browbeating him. It looks like it's a common occurrence.

There's something overtly effeminate about Edward's manner. The way he dresses. The way he carries himself. The way he's checking out every male guest at the reception. It's something Tricia has always refused to see. Or accept.

Edward grabs his glass of Pinot in a huff and joins Loretta and Megan at their table. It's uncomfortable, so Megan gives Loretta the 'say something to him' head bob.

"Having fun, Edward?" asks Loretta.

"A blast," replies Edward, clearly *not* having a blast.

He reaches into his pocket and removes a bottle of white pills. "I guess marrying a nurse is good for something," he mumbles while tossing a few back with the last of his Pinot Grigio. "Can I ask you a question? You're both hospice nurses," he says dryly. "What's it like to watch a person die?"

Loretta and Megan are taken aback, not sure how to respond. Edward clearly doesn't want an answer to the rhetorical question. He looks to the dance floor of men dancing happily with men, and sighs, finishing his thought "because I've been dying a slow death ever since I said, 'I do'."

Megan looks at the bottle of pills still in his hand. "Where'd you get those, Edward?"

"What? These?" he replies quickly and suspiciously, then shoves the bottle back in his pocket. "They're, um, they're just vitamins. You ladies try and have fun. I know I will." And he's off.

"That was weird," says Megan watching him head for the bar.

"Cut him some slack," replies Loretta. "It must be hard being married to Tricia."

Suddenly Davey's head pops up between the two of them. "Wanna know the hardest part about being Edward?" He doesn't wait for their response. "Telling your wife that you're gay."

Megan's mouth drops open. "Shut the front door!"

Davey scoffs, "Oh *please.* Edward is a classic 'still in the closet' kinda gay."

"He is *not* gay," states Megan.

"Wait for it," snarks Davey and makes a bee-line to the DJ Booth.

Tricia approaches the table with two glasses of wine. "Have you seen Edward?" she asks, looking around. "He told me to meet him here with a Pinot."

Loretta replies with pointed sarcasm, "Pinot? You sure he doesn't want something else? Like, a Jack Daniels? Or a Tom Collins?"

Megan gives Loretta a 'stop that' tap on the arm. The inside joke is completely lost on Tricia, as usual.

"I just love weddings," says Tricia looking around the room and joining the table. "Well, traditional ones, anyway. Did you know that the average age for a woman to marry is twenty-seven? That's *exactly* how old I was when I married Edward." She waits, aiming the next line directly at Megan. "You're, what, forty now Megan?"

Megan's fist begins to clench. She thinks, then replies calmly, "Actually, I'm thirty-six. Which is perfect because I always considered myself *way* above average."

Loretta howls with laughter. Tricia deflects the comment, smugly looking around the room, and continues her passive-aggressive observations. "I'm just so happy I found Edward. It's nice to have someone to talk to and to listen. We're perfect together. He's so classy and dignified"

Suddenly, the music blares.

I wanna jitterbug.

Tricia jumps in her seat from the volume.

I wanna jitterbug.

Davey has hijacked the DJ booth and plays WAKE ME UP BEFORE YOU GO-GO by WHAM!

The dance floor erupts into a dancing frenzy. Suddenly, Edward prances across the floor, shouting, "Oh my God. George Michael! I love him!"

Edward is a joyful man possessed, ridiculous and free, having the time of his life surrounded by dancing gay men. Megan shouts to Tricia above the loud '80's music, "Yes. *Very* classy and *super* dignified."

Tricia is mortified. She leaps out of her chair and tries to break through the dance floor to reach her husband, but someone grabs her waist and begins to gyrate. Tricia pulls away in disgust. She is getting bounced around the floor like a pinball as she tries to avoid the dancing frenzy.

Tricia *finally* makes her way to Edward and grabs his ear with a pinch. The crowd cheers and waves 'goodbye' as she drags her husband off the dance floor like a misbehaving child. Megan elbows Loretta, "Well, there they go. The perfect couple."

"Yup," replies Loretta, watching them leave the reception hall. "She helps people die, and *he* wants to."

Megan laughs and sees an opportunity. "Speaking of the perfect couple, Michael and Jackie Boy seem to be getting along."

Loretta nods, "Mmm hmmm."

Megan proceeds cautiously. "You ever talk to Michael at all, you know, about his future?"

"You mean about him wanting to join the Marine Corps?" she replies nonchalantly.

Megan is shocked. "You... you're OK with that?"

"Might be good for him - someday. As long as it's not the Army like his no-good father. Besides, look how good Jackie Boy turned out," she says pointing to the dance floor where Michael is hopelessly trying to teach Jackie Boy how to 'bust a move'. Jackie looks ridiculous. The ladies bust a laugh.

Loretta turns to face her friend with a more serious look. "It's not Michael I'm worried about," she says. "You can't be taking on all these unofficial caseloads. Running all over Boston. Getting wheelchairs and supplies. You're gonna get yourself in trouble."

"If I don't do it, then who the hell will?!" snaps Megan.

Loretta looks her dead in the eye. "We all have a shelf life in this job, Megan. People burn out. I've seen it. Go have some fun, will you? Take a dance class. Learn to paint. Ride a bike."

"I tried that already," Megan deadpans wistfully. "Didn't work out so good."

Loretta pauses, thinking, then says, "That Tim Wallace sure sounds like fun."

"He's married, Loretta," replies Megan in a scolding tone.

Loretta won't have any of it. "Let me ask you something. When's the last time his wife and kid came by?"

Megan doesn't respond.

"All I'm saying is it may *not* be one of those 'happily ever after' kind of marriages," says Loretta full of sass. "Just remember…fifty percent. I'm just sayin'."

SOUTH BOSTON

The dark February sky is clear and full of stars as Megan and Jackie Boy walk arm in arm to their house on M Street, just a short distance from the wedding reception.

"Can I ask you something, Dad?"

"Shoot, kiddo."

"What if Mom were married when you met her?"

"She wasn't," Jackie replies sharply.

"I know. But...but what if she was."

Jackie takes a few more steps before answering.

"World was a lot smaller back then. Simpler. You could tell just by looking at someone's hand."

"Yeah, I know," replies Megan all too knowingly.

"Your mother used to wear her Claddagh ring. Left hand. Heart turned in. Meant you were with someone."

Megan looks at her mother's Claddagh ring that she now keeps on her finger. Right hand. Heart facing out. A painful reminder her that she's available.

"Your mother only did that so creeps like me wouldn't hit on her," Jackie says, only half-kidding.

Megan wraps her arm tighter in his since it's getting cold and starting to snow, softly, big flakes. Winter in New England

"Would you have moved on if mom was with someone? Or did you just know she was the one?"

"The *one?*" Jackie pauses, but only briefly. "Yeah, I guess I did."

"You were lucky, Dad."

"Luck has nothing to do with it," replies Jackie. "You need to work at relationships. People today, they give up on things too easily."

He knows his daughter has something on her mind. He could always sense it. But he doesn't know what to say or how to fix her.

"Here," he stops and hands over a small bouquet of flowers, trying to boost morale. "I fought off two chubby teenagers and an overly aggressive Cougar to catch it for you."

"Thanks. You keep it," she replies with a resigned smile. "I'm gonna hit Murphy's for a nightcap. You wanna join me?"

Jackie Boy looks up to the stars and quickly surveys the street. "The nation is safe. The enemy is quiet. I think this Marine will hit the rack."

Megan smiles, and kisses her dad on the cheek.

"Good night, soldier."

"Semper Fi, little girl."

Megan lovingly looks back at her father as he carries the bouquet of flowers into the house. Two squirrels eat at the feeder. To her surprise Jackie Boy doesn't chase them off.

MURPHY'S LAW - SOUTH BOSTON

Megan sits alone, as usual, and scans the bar filled with tonight's couples sitting close, deep in their Saturday night conversation rituals deciding whether to go home with each other ot not.

And then....shit! There he is. Across the room. The smarmy tanned guy from the other night. Megan ducks her head down behind her shoulder and leans close to the bar.

After a moment, she hears, "How you doin', babe?"

'Babe' now?' she thinks. 'At least he's moved on from Sweetheart and 'Honey.' Through gritted teeth, she stares straight ahead and says, "Why don't you just use a spray tan? It's safer."

"Spray tan? Sounds pretty gay if you ask me."

The voice sounds familiar, and Megan turns to see her ex-boyfriend, Joe Duggan, a blue-collar guy's guy from Southie. A complete 'Mass-hole' through and through. Megan would honestly prefer the smarmy tanned guy.

"Bet there were a lot of spray tans at the gay wedding," says Joe not masking his ignorant arrogance. Megan turns her head around in anger.

"Kevin was your best friend growing up, Joe. You should have been there."

"Yeah, well he should have told me he was into guys," Joe replies defensively. "What did you want me to do, walk him down the aisle?"

"No," Megan says turning her attention back to her beer. "You didn't have to. My father did."

Joe laughs. "Jackie Boy?! I woulda paid admission just to see that."

Megan corrects herself. "Actually, he walked Davey down the aisle. And you never paid for anything." Joe misses the insult. "Well, Davey always did love a man in a uniform. So, how's Kev doin? Seriously."

"He found true love," replies Megan with a hint of jealousy.

"Good for him. So did I," Joe replies and flashes his shiny new wedding ring. Megan rolls her eyes and grabs her date for the night – the bottle of Narragansett beer.

"Tommy," she yells over the bar. "Hit me again over here."

She slaps a $20 down before Tommy can make a comment. Beer in hand, Megan turns to her ex-boyfriend of eight years. "So, what, Joe. You want me to say I'm happy for you?"

"She's pregnant. I did the right thing," he says proudly, as if that makes it all right.

"You're a real Prince, Joe," jabs Megan, then lifts her beer in a mock toast. "Here's to true love...and birth control."

"Don't be like that."

"I was so stupid," Megan says to no one in particular. "I was more in love with the idea of not being alone, than being with you. No worries of us ever affecting the bell curve. We'd have been right up there in that top fifty-percent."

"Fifty percent of what?" asks Joe, completely lost. More than usual.

"Forget it, Joe. You always sucked at math," she says and swigs her beer. "Good luck to you and your future ex-wife."

Joe waits a second before speaking. He knows this is going to hit her between the eyes, but it needs to be said.

"You're a good person Megan. You really are. You deserve to be happy. Not many people could do what you do. But..."

"But what?" she asks, genuinely interested in his answer.

"Your patients. The wakes. The funerals. This bar. You always chose them. Never me."

Megan is stung. Joe tries to soften. "Just needed to be said, is all. Sorry."

He leaves Megan sitting alone, reeling in the truth.

She looks at the oversized brandy snifter full of Mass cards on the shelf behind the bar, evidence of Joe's comment. 'Jesus,' she thinks, 'he was never right about one Goddamn thing during the eight years we dated, and he picks tonight to be right for the first time?!' She pushes her bottle of Narragansett aside.

"Tommy. Whiskey straight. Two fingers," she calls out and opens a wide space between her pinky and index finger, just like Mr. Wallace used to instruct Tim.

Tommy knows the drill and fills a glass.

A voice behind her says, "Anyone sitting here?"

"I'd rather be alone," says a despondent Megan, barely looking up from her drink.

"Nobody wants to be alone," the voice replies.

'Jesus,' she thinks to herself. 'Why the hell do I even leave the house?! Ice cream. Bruins. Bed.'

Thinking the smarmy tanned guy has finally found her, Megan clenches her fist and growls, "Back off pal, or I swear to God I will rip your nuts off."

"They teach you that in nursing school?" the voice asks.

Megan turns, about to swing, and suddenly realizes it's Tim Wallace. Her cheeks glow crimson and she throws a hand over her mouth in embarrassment. "Jesus, Mary and Joseph. Tim, I am so sorry."

Tim is totally amused by the situation. "So, let me see if I have this straight," he begins in a mocking manner. "You know how to both kick nuts in *and* rip nuts off. Very useful skills, you know, under the right circumstances."

She bursts a laugh. "What are you doing here?"

"I worked at a computer company down the Seaport. Used to come here all the time. Mind if I join you?"

She gladly pulls the wooden stool out beside her.

"I love these old dives," Tim says looking around.
"It's one of the few bars left in Southie that doesn't have flat-screen plasma TVs in the bathrooms and avocado on all the sandwiches. Best of all it has puck bowling."

Megan looks at Tim with her signature cocky grin.
"Would you like to lose in that game?"

"You're on."

****

The empty Narragansett beer bottles on the table between them lets everyone know that Megan and Tim have been at this for a while.

"Next time we play skeet ball," slurs Tim, tipsy and tweaked since Megan just kicked his ass, *again,* in puck bowling.

"You're on," she says, and they clink beer bottles.

Tim watches Megan as she takes a long sip from her bottle, noticing how attractive she is. Her brown hair is brushed out and more relaxed with a hint of hereditary Irish red bouncing off the light. The faint blush of makeup highlights her hazel eyes and defined cheek bones.

But there's something else, and it's not just because she's out of those unflattering, un-slimming blue nursing scrubs. Megan is glowing.

"So," asks Tim. "Where were you tonight, all gussied up?"

"A wedding," Megan repliess, then pauses to collect her thought. "Now, let's see if I can explain this. My co-worker Davey married my old boyfriend Joe's best friend Kevin."

Tim tilts his head, confused, like he's taking a complicated math test.

"I know, right," laughs Megan. "And my father gave away the bride. Or the groom. I'm not sure. I just know it wasn't me."

Tim sips his beer. "Ya, well, fifty-percent of all marriages end in divorce."

"Why does *everybody* know that?" Megan says a bit louder than intended. "But I've been thinking. That must mean the other fifty-percent live happily ever after, right?"

"Yeah. I guess you're right," shrugs Tim.

It's Megan's turn to watch Tim finish his beer as a chorus of Catholic guilt voices begin to chatter in her head.

'What are you doing, Megan? Stop. He's married.' But she has so many questions. Like, Why the hell hasn't his wife come to visit Mrs. Wallace? Are they in the unhappy 50% like Loretta said? Part of her doesn't want to know the answer - doesn't care. Megan is drunk. Happy drunk. And for the first time in a long time she's having fun. She thinks to herself, 'Hey Fun Police. Kiss my ass!'

Tim turns to face her in the booth. "The way you are with my mother, you listen like her words are the most important words ever uttered. That's really a special gift."

Megan blushes at the compliment.

"What made you decide to become a nurse?"

"People Magazine," she replies.

He looks at her, dumbfounded. She laughs and tries to explain.

"When I was seventeen, there was an article in People Magazine about Paul Newman and his Hole in the Wall Camp."

"I love his popcorn," declares Tim, a tipsy but serious.

"Paul Newman was an amazing man. So kind and generous. I spent five summers at his camp, working with terminally ill children, helping to give them a different kind of healing. The kids could do anything they wanted, and he would make sure they were all happy in their last days."

Tim looks at her with awe. "So that's why you work in hospice?"

"I wasn't always a hospice nurse," Megan replies. "I used to actually help people get better. Well, medically anyway."

She stares at her drink and begins to pick at the label on her Narragansett bottle.

"When my mother got sick a few years back, we both knew it was bad. But I remembered the kids at camp. How they would come to a sort of peace. They're ready. It's the families who can't let go."

Megan looks at him with determination in her voice and resolve in her eyes. "So, I decided to switch to Hospice. Someone needs to be there to fight for the patients."

"You must have a very strong faith," he says.

Megan raises her glass and toasts in a mocking, almost bitter tone, "Semper Fi, mother fucker."

Megan throws a hand over her mouth. "I'm so sorry. You can take the girl out of Southie, ya know?"

"No worries," smiles Tim. "What's it mean?"

"Mother fucker?" she asks, wide eyed.

Tim spits a laugh. "I know what *that* means! I meant Semper Fi."

"It's from my father," she says with great pride. "He's a Marine. Semper Fi means 'Always Faithful.'"

She stops and thinks for a moment, swirling the words in her head. "Not always," she says, as if she's speaking to herself. She turns and faces Tim. "I'll tell you what I *do* believe. Someone needs to be there to help them cross. Peaceful. Dignified. On *their* terms."

She stares back at her bottle of Narragansett, punctuating her final thought, "No one should die alone."

They both sit in silence as Megan's words hang out there, floating between them. Tim finally breaks the silence.

"Well, I'm sure a lot of folks are happy it was People Magazine that day and not Popular Mechanics."

"Ya, well, I'm pretty good with cars too," brags Megan before pausing, worried she's said too much. "I'm sorry. I've been going on and on."

Tim smiles, "I could listen to your stories all night."

They can't hide the spark between them.

"Those Happy Hours with your mother," says Megan. "It's totally against protocol and pretty much everything I've ever been taught as a nurse. But...they are fun!"

"What? Did I really just hear that?" exclaims Tim dripping with sarcasm. "Is that an admission of fun? I knew you'd come around."

Megan looks right at him. Tim smiles.

"And your Tom Jones impression," she laughs. "Spot on. My mother was crazy for him."

"I do a pretty good Barry White too."

With that, Tim stands up and loudly begins to sing.

Oh baby sweet baby.

Can't get enough of your love baby

Megan grabs him by the hand and pulls him back into the booth. "Are you crazy? Sing a Barry White song in Murphy's?!"

They both laugh, comfortable and easy.

Their hands remain together as they sit side by side, neither letting go, or wanting to. They glance at each other, both not sure of what's really happening.

Tim moves first. A slight lean. Then closer, just about to... but Megan stops him. Something is wrong. Something is different. She looks down at his hand still holding hers and she recoils, thinking to herself, 'How can I be so stupid? He's no better than the smarmy tanned guy!'

With an expression of shock and disbelief, anger and sadness she slides out of the booth.

"Megan, I can explain..."

But he never gets the chance. She's gone.

Tim sits alone.

He reaches into his pocket and slowly slips the wedding ring that had been removed back onto his finger.

(courtesy of larry richardson)

SOUTH BOSTON

Jackie Boy and Michael take their morning jog through the asphalt streets of Southie, chanting back and forth in cadence.

Mile One/ Just for fun

Mile Two/ Good for you

Mile Three/ Good for me

Mile Four/ Let's run some more

Mile Five/ I feel alive

Mile Six/ That's the trick

Mile Seven/ I'm in heaven

Mile Eight/ This feels great

Mile Nine/ I'm feelin' fine

Mile Ten/ Let's run again

One, two, three, four United States Marine Corps.

Oorah!

Michael steps off the curb just as trucks, cars and buses whiz through a busy crosswalk. Rush hour in Boston. A horn blasts! Jackie Boy yanks Michael, instinctively pulling him from harm's way.

"Jesus, kid! You gotta look both ways!"

Michael is breathless and shaken. Jackie tries to deflect responsibility.

"It's…it's not your fault. There should be a sign here. Or at least a Goddamn traffic light or something."

Jackie Boy is always one to survey a situation and suggest rules and improvements, regardless of whether his opinion is asked for or not. They look both ways, about to cross the street together, when a cyclist dressed in an old sweatshirt and sweatpants goes racing by. 'Hmm', Jackie thinks to himself as he eyeballs the rider, 'At least he's not wearin' a goofy neon colored grape-smuggling outfit.'

It's Tim Wallace on his morning route from Beacon Hill through Castle Island.

All clear, Jackie and Michael continue through the crosswalk. They finish their jog on the far edge of Castle Island and stop in front of a military monument of some sort. A large granite stone with a brass inscription stands before them:

Richard Finn

1933 - 1968

Lt. Colonel US Marine Corps

Korea

Vietnam

Jackie Boy looks around with disgust. The area is littered with trash. The stone, surrounded by weeds and dirt, has been defaced with spray paint. The brass is green with patina, weathered from decades of neglect.

"Who is Richard Finn?" asks Michael.

"Dicka Finn," says Jackie Boy. "Toughest Goddamn kid I ever knew. Grew up in the Old Harbor Projects, just up

Day Boulevard there." Jackie points, then begins to reminisce. "I saw Dicka take on a bunch of kids from Dorchester this one time. Four against one. Dicka gave them all a beatin'."

Jackie laughs at the memory.

"The whole neighborhood idolized him. Me especially. Dicka was the first one to call me 'Jackie Boy.' He's the reason I joined the Corps. Well, him and Chesty Puller."

Michael makes a face. "Chesty Puller? Sounds like one of the girls from your magazines."

Jackie Boy points a finger at Michael's chest.

"Don't you disrespect General Lewis B. Puller, the highest decorated Marine in Unites States history."

"Never heard of him," replies Michael, unimpressed.

"But you know all about this Jay-Z fella, right?" scolds Jackie, then turns his attention back to the memorial.

"Used to be that people respected things like medals and plaques more than Gold Records or Grammy Awards, that's for Goddamn sure."

Jackie looks around at the defaced and unkempt area, shaking his head.

"People are so quick to just let things rust and fade away." He removes a hanky from his back pocket, kneels beside the stone and begins to polish the aged brass nameplate best he can.

"Dicka and I served together in Viet Nam. He was a Marine's Marine. He would say, 'these guys don't know they got two kids from Southie over here, Jackie Boy. They don't stand a chance!'"

But Jackie's smile is short-lived. His look changes. His voice gets lower and more measured in tone.

"We were in Khe Sanh. Seven thousand casualties. You'd kill a hundred, another hundred came running at you. I never fought with a braver man."

Jackie pauses to reflect. "Only time I ever seen Dicka scared. And that scared the hell outta me. He got hit. I wanted to get help, but he wouldn't let me."

The painful memories come flooding in.

"'Don't leave me, Jackie Boy. Don't leave me alone.'"

Jackie is trying to hold it together. His voice begins to quiver.

"I sat there and watched my best friend die. I wasn't about to do that again," he says softly, speaking to himself.

"She was alone. Scared and alone. I'm...I'm sure she was calling out my name." Jackie's voice trails off as he tries to mask the tears forming in his eyes.

Michael looks confused and uncomfortable.

"She?" he asks. "What are you talking about?"

Jackie stands up and blows hard into his hanky. Too tough to cry, he begins to collect himself.

"Nothing," he says. "People my age, we can go on and on."

Michael looks up to Jackie with eyes full of admiration and respect, and says, "I could listen to your stories all day."

It's getting cold as the salty sea air whistles in from Boston Harbor. Jackie removes his USMC sweatshirt and hands it to the young boy - a simple gesture that means so much – then turns to face the Finn Memorial. Eyes straight, shoulders back, he stands at attention and snaps a sharp military salute. Michael attempts his own, but the effort is sloppy, the sleeves of Jackie's over-sized sweatshirt dangling at his side.

"What the hell was that?" barks Jackie Boy.

He takes Michael by the shoulders and straightens his position, instructing him the same way he taught Megan when she was that age.

"Let me show you. Now, get your shoulders back. Look sharp, like a soldier. Eyes straight ahead. Straighten that arm and get that elbow up. That's it. Now, raise your right hand until the tip of your forefinger touches your right eye. Thumb and fingers extended. Hand and wrist straight. Make it snap. There you go. Perfect."

Jackie approves. Michael smiles - he belongs to something. The two stand side by side and salute Jackie's fallen boyhood friend.

GIORDANO HOUSE - EAST BOSTON

Megan knocks softly on the bedroom door. Mrs. Giordano's frail voice tells her to enter. Megan can immediately see that the tired woman with the dep caring eyes has begun to fade.

"Is there anything I can do for you Mrs. Giordano?" Megan asks softly, approaching the bedside.

"You can smile for me, Megan," Mrs. Giordano replies, her eyes darker, her hands folded.

"Of course," says Megan. "You always make me smile."

"No. You need to smile on the inside," says the dying woman. Megan looks confused.

"You see my Angelo over there?" smiles Mrs. Giordano. "Always by my side, even when I don't see him, I know he's there. You know what that is?"

"Love," replies Megan with a tender smile.

"Faith," corrects Mrs. Giordano. "You've lost your faith, Megan. I can tell. My boys, they don't always go to church like they should, but they're good boys. They believe. You know what I believe in, Megan? Three F's. Family.

Food. And Faith. Sometimes the order gets mixed up, but you need all three to survive."

Megan looks at her with curiosity, recalling her mother saying something similar.

"But faith. *Sempre Fidele,*" Mrs. Giordano says in Italian. "That's the most important."

"My father was...is a Marine," says Megan full of wonder at the old woman's insight. "I...I don't remember ever telling you about him,"

Mrs. Giordano's tired, knowing eyes look to Megan. "You have family. Plenty of leftovers in my kitchen. That's two out of three F's already."

She takes Megan's hand. "Go find yourself an Angelo to sit by your side, and you'll smile more from the inside."

Mrs. Giordano smiles. It's the knowing smile of an insightful old woman. Megan leans and tucks the blankets in close.

"Grazie, Megan," Mrs. Giordano says softly. "Grazie."

"No," replies Megan with a thin smile. "Thank you."

****

The Giordano boys are at the kitchen table fighting over a tray of lasagna. Megan grabs it away. All three boys begin to protest.

"Hoh!"

"Hey!"

"Whaddya doin'!?"

Megan's grave look lets them know this is important, and that she's in charge. They stop to listen.

"Your mother's blood pressure is low. She's not eating and she's getting dehydrated." Megan continues, knowing it's never easy for loved ones to hear this information. Her tone is professional and caring. "I'll make sure she's comfortable, but I need your help. No arguing. No chaos. We need to give your mother a peaceful crossing."

For the first time all the boys are silent, as if the gravity of their mother's situation finally registers.

"You should start making some arrangements," Megan instructs softly.

Marco, the oldest, speaks first. "She'll want the funeral at DeVito's."

"Where we gonna eat aftah?" asks Silvio.

"Gotta be Marconi's," replies Bruno. "They have the best manicotti."

"No way," says Stevie. "'A Slice of Naples.' The best. And it's Ma's favorite"

"That's not Ma's favorite," pipes Marco.

"Yes, it is," snaps Silvio.

"You're both wrong. It's gonna be..."

Megan steps in to referee before it gets out of hand.

"Stop. Stop it right now. Jesus, no wonder you're all still single."

Silence. Then Bruno mutters under his breath, "Jeeze, what a bitch."

"What?" Megan sneers clenching her fist. "What did you call me?"

"Easy bro," says Marco. "She's from Southie."

Megan opens her mouth to speak, when all of a sudden - *BAM!* A hand comes out of nowhere and slaps Bruno across the face. Everyone looks in stunned silence. It's Mr. Giordano. He has finally left his wife's side.

Bruno hangs his head in shame and apologizes like a scolded child.

"Sorry Megan."

Mr. Giordano's sad eyes turn to Megan, looking for answers. *"Ciò che sta accadendo?"*

Marco puts a hand on his father's shoulder. *"Mamma sta morendo, Papa."*

Megan can see the fear in the old man's eyes. She takes him by the hand. "Your wife is a strong woman who raised four strong sons," she begins. "You need to let her know you're all going to be alright." She looks at Mr. Giordano, tears welling in his eyes. "You need to give her permission to go."

The boys try to absorb the news that their mother may never leave her room alive.

Mr. Giordano bows his head, tears streaking down his wrinkled cheeks as he faces the cruel reality of losing the love of his life - his *'bella ragazza.'*

He returns to the bedroom to tenderly kiss his dying wife goodbye.

HOSPICE CENTER

It's another late night for Tricia as she sits at the desk staring
at her computer, the brightness of the screen bouncing off
her ivory pale skin. The office is neat and tidy, everything
laid out in squares and angles, perfectly coiffed and starched
just like its occupant.

She begins to type.

**As newly appointed Team Lead, it is my pleasure
to announce this year's recipient of the
Compassion Award.**

M E G

Tricia stops, then hits the backspace key to delete the
G leaving just **ME** on the screen. She leans back and rubs
her temples in frustration.

"Yes, it *should* be me!" she says aloud. Her anger gets
interrupted when the phone rings.

"Hello dear. What? Again? That's every night this
week, Edward. I just...I thought we could have dinner
together. Just the two of us."

She looks to the ceiling, listening to another one of
Edward's lame excuses why he won't be home.

"Ok...ok. Fine." She hangs up and stares back at the computer screen.

Tricia never wanted this new leadership role. Edward did. Or rather, Edward wanted the extra money the newly acquired role would pay. He also liked the fact that Tricia would be working longer hours, allowing Edward the freedom to do...well, whatever it is that Edward does when he's not with his wife. It's activity Tricia refuses to think about it.

Truth is, Tricia misses the bedside nursing. The relationships can be so intense, the conversations so meaningful and endless. It's the kind of human interaction Tricia doesn't get in her loveless marriage from her cold, distant, (and according to Davey, gay) husband.

There's a knock at the office door.

"Is...is everything alright, Mrs. Coughlan?" asks Lindsey, her young assistant working late only because Tricia is still there. She has seen Tricia's mood sour whenever the 'I'm not coming home' phone call comes from Edward. A call that seems to happen more often lately.

"Yes. I'm fine Lindsey," says Tricia collecting herself. "What is it?"

"This came for you earlier," Lindsey says dropping an oversized manila envelope on the desk and hurrying out.

Tricia slowly peels open the top. A sinister smile forms across her face.

"Maybe my night isn't ruined after all," she whispers, reviewing the contents.

LOPEZ APARTMENT – ROXBURY

Santiago sits beside his grandfather's bed, a bowl of fresh ice chips in his lap to help keep the old man hydrated. Megan enters the cold, disheveled house. Dishes in the sink. Check. Groceries in the fridge. Check. Red carnation in the vase. Manny was here. Check.

"How's he doing today, Santiago?" she asks.

"Been asleep mostly," he answers, then looks over to Megan.

"Miss Hayes?" asks Santiago with a hint of sadness. "When's my Abuelito going to die?"

Megan doesn't the answer. Medically, no one can predict when a person will die. Megan has seen patients last for days, sometimes weeks - the human will can be a very powerful thing. But an experienced hospice nurse knows when the end is getting near, so they can help prepare the family.

Megan's role is to administer palliative care. She will make sure her patients are comfortable. She will make sure they are free from stress, free from pain, and, most importantly, they are not alone when they cross over. Ever. Not on her watch.

She turns to Santiago, deflecting an answer and just says, "You're doing a real good job, Santiago. Your grandfather is very lucky to have you here, you know that?"

"Yes Ma'am," he replies softly.

After thinking for a moment, he asks, "Miss Hayes. Do you believe in God?"

Megan is stumped for a second time, not sure how to respond.

There *was* a time when Megan believed in God. Twelve years of Catholic school education and a devout Irish mother will do that to you. Megan can't even count the number of masses, wakes and funerals she's been to for the patients in her care over the years. She's certain that 'Masshole' Joe could tell her the exact number, and there's glass snifter full of Mass cards at Murphy's as a constant reminder.

It was her last summer at Paul Newman's Hole in the Wall Camp when Megan first started to question her faith. She always understood the gravity of working with the terminally ill. But, children. Good, kind-hearted children so full of love and hope and promise. How could a benevolent God let this happen?

Megan found some comfort witnessing firsthand how many of the children would find an inner peace near the end. Like she told Tim that night at Murphy's, it's the families that struggle. Mothers and fathers, brother and sisters, sitting in hospital waiting rooms needing something, *anything* to believe in. Megan could see it in their eyes.

Then it happened – the news that her mother had become ill. Gravely ill. And suddenly Megan 'the nurse' became Megan 'the family member', nervously sitting in a hospital waiting room, searching for something, *anything,* to believe in.

Every night, Megan would get on her knees and pray for her mother, just like she did as a child when her father was off fighting a war or traveling overseas.

Then, Polly Hayes got sicker, and Megan's silent prayers just became hollow words.

So, Megan stopped folding her hands and bowing her head and getting on her knees. She grew angry. And that anger burned inside her. And no matter how much she threw herself into work, or mindlessly watched a Bruins game with her father, or drank at Murphy's, or tried to convince herself that she was in love with Joe, she could not rid herself of the anger.

Megan truly can't remember the last that time she prayed. She looks at Santiago, but has no answer to his question.

"I don't know what I believe in anymore," she finally says with a sigh.

"Preacher says you gotta have faith," Santiago replies with a cheery smile.

"So does George Michael," she laughs sadly.

The remark is lost on Santiago. "You wanna know what I believe in?" Megan asks trying to change the subject. "Food. You like Italian?"

She plops down a tray of lasagna that she took from the Giordano's house. Santiago smiles with delight, a man his size is always hungry

Megan join him at the table and looks over at the cartoons playing on TV.

Pepe le Pew is falling in love.

Again.

Le sigh.

SOUTH BOSTON

"Hello?" yells Michael peering through the Hayes back door window. He knocks twice and harder since he's more comfortable at the house. He yells again.

"Hello?"

No response. There to return Jackie Boy's USMC sweatshirt, he figures he might as well open the unlocked door and let himself in.

Michael wanders through the empty house, past Jackie's Lay- Z-Boy recliner, past the tire, weight belt and chain, and stops at the shelf in the dining room that holds Jackie's prized albums. The records are neatly arranged in alphabetical order. Ames Brothers. Bing Crosby. Perry Como. Bobby Darin. 'Of course, they are,' Michael smirks to himself.

He notices the door to Jackie Boy's bedroom is slightly ajar. Looking around to make sure the coast is clear, he tentatively walks in.

Jackie's room is meticulously well kept, the bed made so tight you could bounce a quarter on it. Michael walks up to the dresser and runs his fingers along the smooth polished surface. The mirror sitting atop is wallpapered with photos;

Jackie Boy as a young Marine. Jackie and Polly on their wedding day. A grade school photo of Megan in pigtails, freckles and a missing front tooth.

Just below the mirror, on the far end of the bureau is a small cedar box sitting atop a white lace doily. Michael slowly reaches, then opens it, gently, slowly. His eyes go wide. Inside is a vast assortment of medals, colorful ribbons and pins; an honorary cluster of military recognition that's been awarded to Jackie for his years of service.

Taped to the inside cover of the box is a black and white photo of a beautiful young girl. Michael reaches for it to get a better look.

"Hey! What the hell are you doing there?!"

Michael jumps. Jackie Boy is standing at the doorway.

"I'm sorry. I was just...I..."

"Get out!" bellows Jackie, his face blistering red with anger. "Get the hell out of my house, you little bastard!"

Michael bolts past him, terrified. Something falls from under his arm as he runs through the kitchen and out the back door.

Jackie is completely flustered, and utterly disappointed. He inspects the contents of the cedar box, making sure that everything is intact. It is. He walks to the kitchen and bends to pick up the thin brown paper bag that fell from Michaels arm.

Inside the bag is a brand new, unscratched 45 of Bobby Darin's MACK THE KNIFE.

"Goddamn," Jackie whispers.

QUINCY, MA

Mrs. Wallace is sleeping soundly and peacefully in her own bed. Megan quietly walks in trying not to disturb her. The room is filled with colorful, perfumed flowers that Tim has put there to help cut through the smell of medicines and sickness. As usual, the framed photo of Mr. Wallace is face down. Megan dutifully stands it alongside the others.

"He was a good man," whispers Mrs. Wallace.

"I'm sorry," Megan says softly. "I didn't mean to wake you."

Mrs. Wallace looks at the picture of her husband and sighs. "I'll see him soon enough I guess. The horny toad."

Megan smiles at her sadly, knowingly, and begins to adjust the pillows to make her patient more comfortable.

"Let's not talk like that now."

"You seem tired, Megan," says Mrs. Wallace. "Come. Come sit with me."

Mrs. Wallace is weakening. Megan can see death forming like storm clouds in her eyes and the look reminds her of her own mother.

"There's something about this terrible disease," Mrs. Wallace says slowly, deliberately. "How it inflicts people. It doesn't care if you're dirt poor, or a rich, famous movie star, or just a tired old lady. It keeps you up at night, thinking of all the good things out there that you can't enjoy...and you begin to cry. You curse and get angry that it ever found you."

Megan agrees, "Cancer is a terrible disease."

"Oh no, Megan," says Mrs. Wallace. "I never cried because I got cancer. Cancer just floats around and lands on people. It landed on me."

The old woman looks deeply at Megan, holding her gaze steady. "I'm talking about loneliness. That stops more hearts than any cancer ever could. It's just a shame people don't realize it."

Megan nods lovingly and takes Mrs. Wallace by the hand.

The tender moment is interrupted.

"Buongiorno! Who wants to go to Italy today?" Tim sings, oblivious to the mood in the room. He's dressed like an Italian Organ Grinder. Red striped shirt, Fedora hat. A thick black mustache glued to his upper lip. Strapped to his chest is an old-fashioned accordion, with a cymbal clanging toy monkey perched on top. The monkey is regally outfitted in gold chains and a blue silk shirt.

Megan stands abruptly. "I'm sorry. I have to go."

"But you just got here," pleads Mrs. Wallace.

"I know. I'm sorry," Megan tells her. "Actually, I...I have a date." Mrs. Wallace and Tim look surprised by the announcement. A date? Really? Tim's not sure how to react.

Megan does her best to avoid eye contact. She's still pissed off from their night at Murphy's. It's awkward.

"Don't you like Italian?" Tim asks, trying to get her to look in his direction.

"I seriously doubt it," she says on her past.

The mechanical monkey claps and clangs its toy cymbals as Tim watches Megan rush out the door and down the hall.

THE NORTH END

Candles flicker in Chianti bottles, the wax dripping down onto red and white checkered tablecloths inside one of the scores of Italian family-style restaurants littered throughout Boston's historic North End. Men and women drown in gold jewelry, spray tan, hair product, and the finest Italian shoes to ever fall off the back of a truck.

Bruno Giordano sits in a booth in the back corner picking his teeth with a matchbook cover. He sees Megan at the entrance and eagerly waves her over. Pausing at the door, Megan takes a deep breath and readies herself, glancing skywards as if to say, 'God help me.'

She slides into the booth and eyes Bruno's outfit up and down. He's wearing a gaggle of gold chains and his hideous blue silk shirt - the exact same outfit as Tim's toy monkey.

"Nice shirt," she says with a laugh.

"I know. Pretty sweet, right?" he replies and immediately slides over. Megan pushes him back.

The owner and chef, Freddie, approaches the table to take their order. He's wearing a lined, weathered Mediterranean face and a white apron splattered with red 'gravy' and oils.

"I'll have a Narragansett," says Megan. "And get Curious George over here a Banana Daiquiri."

"Che cos'è Narragansett?" the owner asks Bruno, confused.

"It's a beer," Bruno tells him. "Just bring me the usual, Freddie."

Freddie walks away, scowling with disgust. A beer? The Pagliuca family came to this country from Avellino, bringing old family recipes to cook the best Italian food in Boston. Red house wine is the requisite, and this woman is going to complement his food, his mother's food, his grandmother's food with …what did she call it? Narragansett?!

"*Minga*," Freddie curses under his breath in Italian as he returns to the kitchen.

Bruno slides in closer to Megan. Again. She pushes him back. Again. Only this time it's more of a shove.

"Settle down," she tells him. "I'm only doing this as a favor to your mother. Capisce?"

Megan looks around the restaurant at the brick walls stacked with wine and plastic vines. "So, they have puck bowling in this place?"

Now it's Bruno's turn to scowl with disgust. "Puck bowling? No. They got Keno."

Freddie arrives with a plate overflowing with salami, prosciutto, sautéed mushrooms, and cheese, and sets the oversized antipasto on the table. Bruno immediately grabs his napkin and tucks it neatly under his chin to carefully protect the front of his prized blue silk shirt. He leans back and stretches his arms along the top of the booth, waiting for Megan to serve him.

"You can't be serious," she says, and slides out to leave.

"No, no. Wait," pleads Bruno, his eyes looking at the door. "Hold on. Here she comes."

Into the restaurant walks Dorothy Manganaro. Well, not so much walks in. She storms in like a hurricane. Dottie is a force. Lots of hair. Lots of makeup. Lots of gum. Lots of attitude. She barrels over to the booth.

"What's this, Bruno? She your girlfriend now?!" Dottie yells between snaps of gum.

"No, no. It ain't like that, babe," replies Bruno, his secret plan to get her jealous set in motion. "This here's my mother's nurse."

"Then why you all dressed up?" she asks. "Got your classy blue shirt on and everything."

Bruno bobs his head at Megan as if to say, 'see, I told you it's a great shirt!'

"It's not what you think, Dottie," pleads Bruno. "She's Irish, for cryin' out loud."

"Yeah?" snaps Dorothy glaring down at Megan. "Well, this ain't Southie, sweetheart."

Megan has had enough. In her thickest Irish brogue, she stands up and says, "No it 'tisn't. Makes me long for the old country, though."

With the whole restaurant looking on, she yells, "Come on, lads. Sing with me!"

Oh Danny Boy

The pipes, the pipes are calling

From glen to glen

and down the mountain side.

Bruno grabs her by the hand and pulls her back into the booth. "Are you crazy? Sing an Irish song in Pagliuca's?!"

Megan cuts her losses. "He's all yours, sweetheart. Monkey shirt and all." She slides from the booth, and heads for the door.

Once outside, Megan looks back through the restaurant window to see Dorothy spoon-feeding Bruno his antipasto. They are perfect for each other. It's the beginning of another love story. Just not Megan's

She pulls the collar up on her heavy wool coat and walks out into the cold Boston night.

Alone.

Websters Dictionary defines loneliness as:

 1.) Being without company.

 2.) Not frequented by other human beings

 3.) Sad from being alone.

 4.) Producing a feeling of bleakness or desolation.

But life isn't always so easily defined.

Snow falls over Boston's dark city skyline as;

 -Megan steps off the bus from her disastrous 'date' with Bruno, and slowly walks along the cold cement sidewalks of South Boston.

- Jackie Boy stares out his living room window at the untouched snow shovel leaning against his house.

- Angelo Giordano keeps silent vigil by his dying wife's bedside.

- Santiago Lopez sits beside his ailing grandfather. He shakes pills from a medicine bottle onto the nightstand and begins to grind them with a spoon into white powder.

- Michael Evans stands across the street from the Hayes house, silently watching as the snow piles up on the front steps.

- Tim Wallace sits at an easel in the playroom of his empty apartment. He fills in the colors of a painting that looks like it was done by a child.

- Tricia Coughlan places a plastic container into the small microwave in her office, sadly watching the carousel spin her dinner-for-one.

They are all struggling with their own version of loneliness.

Maybe Mrs. Wallace was right.

SOUTH BOSTON

The oversized Chevy Chrysler is parked across from the Hayes house. Charlie drinks coffee - black. Jeremy drinks tea - herbal.

"Maybe you could start small. A walk after dinner. A slow jog. Yoga maybe?" says Jeremy.

"Ya, that's it. Yoga," replies Charlie with a biting tone. "Tight stretchy pants. Headband. Rolling on the floor in a room full of women. Trying like hell not to fart. Perfect."

"If sarcasm was an exercise, you'd be in great shape," replies Jeremy.

"I'm getting too old for any of that workout shit," Charlie says as he pulls a huge submarine sandwich from a brown paper bag.

"It's never too late to change your life," says Jeremy in his best inspirational-quote-of-the-day voice.

Charlie nudges his partner to look toward the Hayes front door.

Jackie Boy steps off the front porch into the new winter snow and lets the cold grey morning air fill his lungs.

He descends the steps, wraps the weight belt around his waist and begins to slowly jog, dragging the chain and tire behind him. Jeremy immediately glares at Charlie as if to say, *you're too old?!*

"Namaste, dickhead," says Charlie as he bites into the meatball sub, the sauce falling onto a stomach that is spilling over his belt.

A hulking figure approaches the Hayes front stoop. Jeremy grabs the camera, points and shoots.

Click. Santiago Lopez stands at the Hayes front door.

Click. His hand in a pocket.

Click. Megan opens the door.

Click. Santiago removes a bag of pills.

Click. Megan looks up and down the street.

Click. Santiago is ushered into the house.

MBTA STOP - SOUTH BOSTON

"N.G.," says Jackie Boy.

"J.B.," replies the driver.

It's the abbreviated salutation exchanged every morning between the Chinese-American bus driver and it's Southie-Irish Marine Corps passenger.

Jackie climbs on board, making his way down the center of the bus, and takes a seat. Two elderly women board at the first stop. Ever the chivalrous soldier, Jackie Boy stands to give them his seat.

The women giggle like smitten school girls. 'Oh yeah,' Jackie thinks to himself with a cocky, shit-eating grin. 'I still got 'Game' with the ladies.'

Suddenly, loud music blares from his USMC sweatshirt.

I got 99 problems but a bitch ain't one

The women are appalled and lean away.

If you havin' girl problems I feel bad for you son

I got 99 problems but a bitch ain't one

Flustered, Jackie jumps to search for the source, and finally locates Michael's iPhone that was left in the pocket of sweatshirt. He fumbles to turn off the loud music, then attempts to get his 'Game' back with the ladies.

"Sorry about the language, ladies. That's, ah, that's Jay-Z."

The ladies are unimpressed.

Jackie tries to explain. "One of the most successful rapper guys?"

Nothing.

"He was married to Doris Day. Or was it Nanette Fabray? Christ, I can't remember."

The bus stops, and the ladies stand up and leave. Jackie's 'Game' is over. He slumps into the seat and looks down at the cold, wet tire propped against his leg. Maybe Megan is right. Maybe he should get a job at Walmart handing out smiley stickers.

Jackie did his twenty years in the military and received an Honorable discharge with a small pension. But his restlessness in 'retirement' would never allow him to sit still for very long. And neither would Polly.

So, when a buddy from the Service offered him a job as a Pressman for the Boston Globe, he jumped at the chance. His military training helped him excel working on the large iron machines, some as big as four stories tall, in an environment that needed to run on time, and in order.

Every morning at sunrise, after his 50 pushups and 50 sits ups, he would make his way down Morrisey Boulevard, rain, sleet or snow to The Globe. Jackie always got a kick watching the rich kids from the suburbs exit the MBTA and navigate the early morning ice on the Columbia Point footbridge as they rushed to get to their first class at BC High. He would bark orders to the pimply-faced freshmen, "Set your alarms, gentlemen! You never want to be later than ten minutes early." Every young man is a fresh recruit to Jackie Boy Hayes.

Jackie worked at the Globe for thirty years. But then the early 2000's hit - a time when even fishing and coal mining weren't losing jobs as fast as the newspaper industry. Print wasn't dead, but it was certainly on life support. It seemed that no one under forty was reading a physical newspaper anymore.

So, the machines that had been running daily since 1958 suddenly stopped, and Jackie Boy was an idle civilian. Again.

The bus slows to a stop. Jackie Boy stands, grabs the weight belt, chain and tire, and makes his way out into the brisk wintry morning. The printing machines at the Boston Globe may have stopped running, but Jackie Boy Hayes isn't about to. Ever.

****

The snow had fallen heavily throughout the night and early morning making Jackie Boy's progress to Castle Island less certain. Nevertheless, he follows the usual path along the edges of Boston Harbor. Head down, chain and tire in tow, Jackie Boy begins his slow jog through the park without his running partner since hasn't heard from or seen Michael for days - not since he ran terrified and ashamed out the back door of the kitchen.

Jackie jogs through the park and turns a corner behind a small patch of trees. Suddenly the three teenage punks from the bus incident jump out and surround him. He stops in his tracks.

"Well, well, if it isn't the Andrews sisters. LaVerne. Maxene. And you must be *Patty*," he says condescendingly to the toughest one. "Listen kids, if you plan to hit, hit hard...because I only swing once. Ballgame."

The punks are a bit taken aback by the old man's confidence.

From out of nowhere comes a primal, virile scream.

"OORRAAAHH!"

Michael appears swinging the snow shovel.

BAM! He hits one of the punks on the head. The second punk knocks Michael to the ground.

BOOM! Jackie Boy clocks the attacker square on the jaw, breaking it in two with a right hook that would have made Dicka Finn proud. Ballgame.

The lead punk pulls a knife from his jacket and presses the blade against Jackie's throat. They all stop. Jackie and the punk stare nose to nose in long hostile silence. The situation could go either way judging from the intensity. Then, for the first time in his life, Jackie Boy decides to stand down.

"Cut him, bro," yells the punk holding his broken jaw. The leader slowly and with intimidation takes the knife and begins to cut at Jackie's shirt, just below the neck. He stops when he sees a green USMC symbol tattooed on the top of Jackie's chest. Below the insignia are words in Latin.

"What the hell is that?" asks the punk.

"In Omnia Paratus," replies Jackie, his voice beaming with strength and pride. "it means 'ready for anything.'"

The punk is impressed. "You used to be a Marine?"

"He *is* a Marine!" Michael yells from the ground.

The punk's demeanor changes. "My brother is 2nd Battalion 9th Marines. Afghanistan."

"Task Force Leatherneck," states Jackie. "Good men in that unit." The combatants' eye each other up and down for a moment.

"Let 'em go," the punk tells his sidekicks standing over Michael. Then he leans in close and whispers to Jackie. "Maybe you can show me that wrist move some time."

Jackie looks him in the eye. "There's always a bus leaving for Parris Island, kid. Might make a man out of you."

The punk gives a nod out of respect, then motions to his defeated sidekicks for them to takeoff.

All clear, Jackie Boy bends to pick up his tire, and suddenly falls to the ground, grimacing and writhing in pain.

"Goddamn it to hell!"

Michael rushes to his side. "What's wrong?"

"Listen to me kid. Are you listening?" whispers Jackie Boy.

"Yes, Sir. I'm right here," says Michael, terrified.

"Can you hear me?" asks Jackie, grabbing Michael by the shirt.

"What is it Jackie Boy?" he asks, not knowing what to do or how to help. "Is it your heart?"

"You need to promise me something," gasps Jackie, his breathing heavy and labored.

"Anything Jackie. Anything."

"There's a box in the back of my closet," Jackie says, then pauses for dramatic affect. "Megan can never find it."

"Is it something special?" asks Michael trying his best not to panic. "Something from the war?"

"Yeah," grins Jackie Boy. "My girlie magazines."

Michael finally realizes he's being duped. "What? You want me to get rid of your porn?"

"It's classic stuff from the 60's and 70's. There are things in there you can't *unsee*, kid. Would rock your world."

Jackie forces a chuckle. Michael shakes his head. "You're crazy, old man."

"It's just my back. Help me up," says Jackie, laughing. Michael grabs the tire and the two turn to head for the bus stop.

"I'm serious about those magazines, kid," says Jackie Boy out the side of his mouth. "That's an order."

192

DUDLEY SQUARE, ROXBURY

Megan stands on the front steps of the Lopez apartment complex. She looks tired and stressed. Loretta is right- all those extra unofficial caseloads, running around Boston getting wheelchairs and groceries for patients is really taking its toll. The cell phone inside her coat buzzes. Megan looks at the screen.

TIM WALLACE

She ignores the call and turns the key to open the door, but the bolt is locked from the inside preventing her from entering. 'That's odd,' she thinks, 'Santiago never bolts the door.' She knocks. After a moment, the seedy-looking thug in a black do-rag opens the door a crack.

"Who are you?" he asks, his eyes suspiciously darting up and down the hallway.

"I'm Mr. Lopez's nurse," snaps Megan with authority.

"He don't need no nurse no more," says the thug trying to close the door, but Southie-tough Megan pushes past him. She makes her way to Mr. Lopez who is lying still in bed. She checks his vitals. The old man has crossed over.

"Were you with him when he died?" Megan asks the seedy thug now standing over her.

"What?"

"Was he alone?" she asks. "Where is Santiago?"

Her eyes dart around the room and land on the glass vase beside the sink. It's empty. No red carnation. Manny hasn't been home either.

"Santiago ain't here," says the thug, his tone threatening.

Her cell phone buzzes. Megan looks.

TIM WALLACE

She ignores his call again. Her suspicions rise. She moves toward the nightstand of pill bottles, but the thug stops her.

"I need to properly dispose the medications," she tells him.

The thug moves towards her. "You ain't disposin' nothing," he says through gritted, yellowed teeth.

Her cell phone buzzes again.

TIM WALLACE

"I...I need to answer this," she says, her tough Southie demeanor rapidly changing to fear. The thug grabs her by the arm. "You need to find me those pills!" he growls, shoving her into the nightstand. Empty pill bottles scatter to the floor.

Suddenly, the front door swings open and Santiago fills the room. Seeing Megan in distress, his face turns dark and furious. He swiftly grabs the intruding thug by the neck and lifts him off his feet. Megan tries to stop him.

"Santiago! Let him go. Let him go!"

But it's no use. Santiago is a man possessed, practically choking the thug to death.

Megan pleads with him. "Santiago," she says as calmly as she can. "You need to let him go."

Slowly, reluctantly, Santiago releases his grip as the thug struggles to breathe, his feet finally touching down. Gasping for air, the thug quickly darts out the open front door.

Santiago walks to his grandfather's bedside, slowly and calmly, as if nothing happened. He reaches to his back pocket to retrieve a cross of Jesus and gently places it on the dead man's chest.

"I'm sorry I wasn't here to let you in, Miss Hayes," he says. "I...I had to go to Church."

Megan is still shaking. She puts her hand on Santiago's shoulder. "I'm so sorry, Santiago. I really thought your grandfather had more time."

"He's in heaven with Mama, right?" he asks seeking her confirmation.

"Yes, I believe he is."

"That's good," says the gentle man-child looking at his grandfather lying peacefully in bed. Megan tries her best to console him. "You did a great job, Santiago. You were always here."

Santiago turns and looks at Megan. "I'm sorry about showing up at your house like that the other day, Miss Hayes. When I dropped the medicine box, I didn't know which pill was SpongeBob time and which pill was Road Runner time. I...I just put them all in a bag and came over."

"It's fine," says Megan, with a sad smile. "You're welcome anytime."

Santiago is quiet and begins to rock gently back and forth. Megan can see that something is troubling him. He finally speaks, but in measured tones.

"Mi abuelito...he seemed really uncomfortable. More than usual. Lotsa groanin'. A dog gets like that they put 'em down, right?" Santiago says, as if justifying the confession. He can't take his eyes off his beloved grandfather.

"He got to see the trees, though, right Miss Hayes? Even with the snow on them, they still had life." He turns to Megan. "Thank you, Miss Hayes."

Megan crouches down and begins to collect the empty pill bottles from the floor. Placing them on the nightstand, she notices the spoon and residue of crushed powder. It all makes sense to her now.

"Are you gonna be in trouble, Miss Hayes?" asks Santiago.

Megan looks at him and sighs, "I'll figure something out."

Her cell phone buzzes again.

TIM WALLACE

HAYES HOUSE - SOUTH BOSTON

Michael and Jackie Boy sit at the kitchen table, two warriors enjoying soft drinks after their scuffle in the Park.

"That tattoo of yours is pretty cool, old man...I mean, Sir," Michael says, correcting himself. Jackie Boy looks to his chest and rubs a finger along the faded green ink.

"Ready for anything," he recites, but the words fall flat. "Not everything," he whispers back.

Michael leans back in his chair, feeling pretty cocky about himself, seeing as he just saved Jackie Boy's life and all.

"I'm thinking of getting one," Michael says cracking open another bottle of soda as if he were sharing a beer with a fellow soldier after battle. Jackie frowns. "Negative. You're not getting any ink until you're at least twenty. Maybe twenty-five. Now sit up straight!"

The chair slides. Michael bolts upright.

Realizing he was a bit harsh, Jackie softens. "Make your mark on another person first. That's all."

Michael takes that in and nods, then timidly looks across the table. "I'm sorry about the other day. I shouldn't have been in your room."

"No, you shouldn't have," Jackie replies. They both sit, staring at the soda bottles in front of them. One thing Jackie Boy Hayes would never tolerate in his own troops was low morale. So, he stands up and heads off to his room to find a remedy for the situation.

Michael shifts in his seat when he sees Jackie returning with the cedar box that sits atop the dresser, thinking to himself, 'Oh boy, here it comes.'

Jackie opens the box slowly, deliberately, the aroma of wood mixed with the faint smell of perfume. On the back cover sits the black and white photo of a beautiful young girl. Polly Hayes.

Michael can see Jackie's tough exterior beginning to melt away. The battle tested Marine in that moment is a husband, a father, and a lonely widower.

"Your wife," Michael says softly. "She was really pretty."

"That is affirmative, kid," says Jackie Boy tracing a thumb along the curled edge of the photo, breathing in her memory. "That is affirmative."

Jackie collects himself and looks Michael square in the eye.

"I have something for you."

His hand reaches into the box and pulls out a silver medallion dangling from a chain. "Mrs. Hayes gave this to me when I shipped overseas."

Michael takes the medal in his palm and looks closely.

"Saint Michael. Defender in battle," he says with wonder and gratitude. Jackie stands and repeats the words as he places the medal around the young boy's neck. "Saint Michael. Defender in Battle."

The boy beams with pride. "Thank you, Sir."

Neither of them speak, both wanting to enjoy the moment. Then, slowly, Michael's mood changes. Something is wrong.

"What's the matter," asks Jackie. "Don't you like it?"

"No, it's just...the snow's almost gone. You probably won't need me around anymore."

Jackie looks to the window. "I could probably use someone to police the area in the Spring. Wash the sidewalk. Clean the gutters."

"It'll be a good work out, right?" Michael says grinning.

"Roger that," Jackie replies, smiling back at his young friend. He stands and exclaims, "I'll make us some chow."

Michael bounces into the living room and plops himself deep into Jackie's Lay-Z-Boy recliner, like he's been ordained the man of the house.

"Whoa! Whoa! Whoa!" yells Jackie. "What the hell are you doing? We eat at the table, soldier!"

Michael immediately stands and makes his way back.

"We got two rules in this house. Candles with every meal. And music. There's always music, Mikey Boy."

With that, Jackie walks to the living room for his prized music collection. He reaches to the shelf and slides a record from its sleeve. Then, to Michael's surprise, Jackie Boy hands him the album, allowing the boy to carefully, *gingerly* drop the needle.

After a pop and a scratch, Dean Martin begins to croon.

> *Everybody finds somebody sometime*
> *There's no telling where love may appear*
> *Something in my heart keeps saying*
> *My someplace is here*

QUINCY, MA

Megan rushes into Mrs. Wallace's bedroom, still rattled from her experience at the Lopez apartment just a few hours earlier.

"I'm so sorry I'm late," she says hurriedly taking off her hat and coat. "Tim was calling me, but I had to wait at another..."

Megan stops in her tracks. Her eyes stare at the nightstand. The framed photo of Mr. Wallace is standing upright and untouched. Megan looks to the bed.

"Mrs. Wallace? Mrs. Wallace!"

The tired, kind woman has crossed over.

Tim is behind her. "Megan. I...I tried calling you."

Megan is a mess, about to lose it. "Was...was she alone?"

"I was here," Tim says softly, as if that might help. It doesn't. Megan runs from the room, unraveling. Tim catches her in the hallway and holds her close. She falls into his arms, sobbing deeply into his shoulder. Their eyes meet in a mixture of sorrow, confusion, and loneliness.

After a moment, Megan pulls away and composes herself. Like her Marine Corps father, she has her duties.

With a Tricia-like coldness, Megan straightens her smock, dries her eyes, and gathers herself into a woman in control. A *nurse* in control.

"Call the Funeral Home," she says with cold professionalism. "I need to prepare the body."

She heads back to the bedroom to be with her patient.

HAYES HOUSE - SOUTH BOSTON

Night falls over Southie as Megan sits at the kitchen table with a bottle of Dewar's for company. She's deeply unsettled by the day's events.

Jackie climbs the basement stairs to make his nightly protein shake. He could always tell when a battle was about to erupt, it's a gut feeling he gets deep inside whenever he was in enemy territory. He knows there's a storm brewing on the home front, right there in the kitchen, so he gets battle ready and goes on the offensive.

"Why don't you give your elbow a rest. Looks like you've been halfway around the world there already," he says looking at the shot glasses from Germany, Japan, Thailand and Spain lined in front of Megan.

He begins to mix a protein shake of powders, kale, broccoli and flax seed. It's brown and disgusting. The whir of the blender only intensifies Megan's sour mood and she pours herself another shot of whiskey (this time in a glass from South Korea). Megan can see the disapproval in her father's eyes. But she doesn't care.

"You drink your brown drink. I'll drink mine," she says, downing the shot and giving him a sloppy salute.

"What's with you?" Jackie asks. "No Happy Hour with the old bag today?"

"Mrs. Wallace is dead," replies Megan coldly. "But I'm sure you'd be there for her if she needed you, Dad."

"What the hell is that supposed to mean" he asks. "I didn't even know the woman."

Megan doesn't respond. She pours another one (this time Cuba), well on her way to getting drunk.

"You should have taken that promotion," Jackie finally confronts her. "Nice office job. Normal hours. It would've got you away from all the sickness for a while. All that death."

"Maybe I should've just worked at the Globe," Megan replies. "Or maybe I should have been a tough, cold Marine - like you."

Silence hangs in the room. Jackie waits for a moment to collect his thoughts before speaking.

"I never pretended to be anyone else, Megan. I was preparing you for life, raising you tough so you could face a tough world. You think you could've handled all this hospice business without it? You surround yourself with death every day."

"And you run from it," she snaps, delivering the words like a punch to the gut. Megan looks at him, the pain of the past finally unearthed -- for both — and finally busts.

"Where were you, Dad? Huh? Where were you?"

Jackie Boy sits down, tired and defeated.

"I…I don't want to fight, Megan. Not tonight."

But Megan doesn't stop, she's been holding it in too long. Something inside her feels like it's come untethered.

"*Now* you don't wanna fight?! You fought Mom when she said she was too tired to go on! You fought the doctors when they said they've done all they can! You fought me when I wanted to bring hospice in!"

Jackie explodes, the emotion spewing out. "You and your Goddamn hospice. You're all so quick to give up. A Marine never retreats! Never surrenders!"

"She wasn't a recruit! She was your wife!" cries Megan. "I knew what she wanted, what she *needed* but you wouldn't let me help her. She didn't have to suffer…"

"Enough, Goddamn it! Enough!" screams Jackie Boy, slamming his fist on the table, the anger bursting like steam from a furnace. "You don't think I drag that pain around every day? Every single God Damn day! I stood outside that door, watched you care for her night after night after night. I heard her. I wanted to be there...I just...I..."

Jackie's voice trails off in despair.

After a moment of dead silence, Megan speaks. "She made me leave to go find you. She died alone. I can never forgive myself for that. Or you."

Megan stands and runs from the room, the tears flowing out of her.

Jackie Boy sits alone, speechless, staring into the candle flames as they flicker on the kitchen table.

And then it happens - something that has never happened before. John Donald 'Jackie Boy' Hayes, defender in battle, a Marine's Marine, a soldier who represents fearlessness and bravery and relentless drive, lays his head on his powerful arms, and begins to cry.

HOSPICE CENTER

"Good morning," chirps Loretta as she enters the lunchroom. Megan is seated at the table and quickly grabs a nearby newspaper to conceal her face. Loretta pours herself a coffee and glances in Megan's direction. "You reading the Classifieds?"

"Shopping for a cat," replies Megan almost too quickly.

Something is wrong. The maternal instinct in Loretta can feel it. She sits beside her friend and waits. Megan drops the paper and finally breaks down, sad and frustrated and hungover.

"I try, Loretta. I try *so* hard to be there, but it's useless," she says burying her head and sobbing deeply into her friend's shoulder. "My father is right. We all die alone. And I'm scared, Loretta. I'm so scared that I'm going be alone."

Loretta holds her close, rocking her friend gently back and forth. "Oh Megan. What did I tell you the first day you started here? Watch carefully. The patients will teach you how to live. You just have to listen."

Loretta wipes the tears from Megan's red puffy eyes.

"You remember my patient Miss Callahan? She was a teacher in Watertown for thirty-five years. Never married. No children. Day before she passed, she sits up in her bed. 'Look, Loretta,' she says. 'You see them? The children. All the children are here.' Damn if she didn't see all her students right there at the foot of her bed."

Loretta takes Megan's face in her hands and looks her in the eye. "No one dies alone, Megan. No one *ever* dies alone."

They hug, and everything in the world seems as though it will be alright.

"And I'll tell you something else," says Loretta. "You become one of those crazy white ladies with thirty cats and I can promise you won't die alone. I'll be standing right there over your dead body."

She pulls back and looks at her friend. "Cuz I'll kill you myself."

Megan finally smiles.

Tricia barges in, interrupting the tender moment.

"Megan. You're needed in the Conference room immediately."

****

Megan enters a stately, ominous conference room with chairs lining both sides. Dr. Powers is seated at the far end between two men that Megan doesn't recognize. One man is heavyset and disheveled, the other man is neatly dressed and painfully thin. She immediately doesn't like either one of them.

"Megan. Please have a seat," begins Dr. Powers as calmly as he can. After a moment of uncomfortable silence, he continues. "This is a bit delicate. It has been brought to our attention that the dispensary inventory is off."

Her shoulders slump. She's busted.

"The Lopez pills. I know. I realize that my count was off, but I can explain."

Thin guy Jeremy speaks up. "Miss Hayes, are you aware that Mr. Lopez lives in a high drug trafficking area?"

Megan shoots him a look, her Southie toughness shifting into gear. "Yeah, well cancer doesn't check zip codes," she says with a tone as sharp as a switchblade.

It's overweight Charlie's turn to speak up. Megan does her best to avoid staring at his hideous combover.

"Your medication count was also off after visiting the Lopez family on the," he looks to his notepad, "11th and 12th."

"I've been very clear about my counts," says Megan, looking directly at a visibly uncomfortable Dr. Powers.

"Could you explain this?" asks Jeremy, as he slides a thick manila envelope across table for effect. He is loving every minute of the Super Cop drama. Megan peels the top open and spills pictures onto the table.

Santiago Lopez at her front door.

His hand in a pocket.

A bag full of pills.

Megan at her front door.

Megan ushering Santiago into the house.

"What? How did you...?" she asks, her voice a mixture of anger and confusion.

Jeremy continues his interrogation. "There's been quite a number of urban youths coming in and out of your house lately."

Megan's fist begins to clench. "By urban youths, do you mean Michael? That's Loretta's son. He's been helping my father."

"Yes, your father," says Charlie, his hands folded across his huge stomach. "Interesting character, your father is. Jogs all over South Boston dragging a tire. Bad back and all."

Megan's head is spinning. Fat Charlie continues, his tone full of accusation. "You think he might like a little help? You know, for the back pain?"

Megan glares at them, her fist is now a tight ball of fury. She turns to Dr. Powers. "Stan, what the hell is this all about?"

Megan is confident enough in her skills, her reputation, and her work history to address Dr. Powers as Stan, and frankly at this point she really doesn't give two shits about protocol.

"All my meds are accounted for," she tells them. "Every last pill. You can check with Tricia."

Dr. Powers looks visibly uncomfortable. He never wanted this meeting. The whole situation was forced on him.

He looks at the open envelope sitting on the table in front of them with sad resignation.

"We already have."

Megan flips the envelope over to see the name written on the front:

Tricia Coughlan.

Dr Powers continues. "Once Mrs. Coughlan was aware of the dispensary issue, she took it upon herself to hire these gentlemen and launch a private investigation."

Megan is reeling.

"This is all so very disappointing," Dr. Powers says with a genuine sadness. He adjusts himself, sits up straight, and goes into full CEO administrator mode.

"Mrs. Coughlan has graciously agreed to work with your patients until a review committee can be established. You may want to speak with her about the transition."

"The 'transition', huh?" Megan says with a mocking tone only half listening, her eyes haven't left the surveillance photos. "Is that what we're calling it?"

HOSPICE CENTER

Tricia sits alone in the lunch room, as always. The door swings open and in walks Davey. He gives her a forced, fake smile, and with nowhere else to sit joins her at the table.

It's always an interesting dynamic when these two are in the same room. Her passive aggressive homophobia and his blatant disdain for her authority (and her poor fashion choices) always make for a combustible setting.

Davey removes a plastic baggy of carrot sticks from his Patridge Family lunch box. It's sort of his 'thing' – finding retro metal lunch boxes from the 70's and 80's in shops and yard sales all over Boston. Today's food is neatly stored in a 'Partridge Family' lunchbox shaped like their multi-colored school bus.

He starts eating the carrot sticks, biting loudly and slowly just to bust Tricia's balls, of which Davey firmly believes that she has two. And they are huge. The sound of crunching carrots fills the room with quiet tension.

"So," Davey asks, finally breaking the silence. "Did Eddie have fun at the wedding?"

Tricia glares. "It's Edward. And yes, thank you. It was a fine time."

"Oh, I'm sure Eddie had a *gay* old time," says Davey biting his lip to stifle a laugh. Before Tricia can say anything, the doors burst open and Megan storms in.

"You lying, self-righteous bit..."

But Megan stops herself. Tricia responds in her typical cold Nurse Ratched-like fashion, "I was just doing my job."

"And I've been doing mine!" snaps Megan getting right up in Tricia's grill. "Don't you *ever* question my integrity."

Tricia stands to defend herself and wrestle back authority. "I am not questioning your integrity, Megan. I'm questioning your responsibility. Your leadership skills. Your...your..." She struggles to find the words. Down deep, Tricia knows Megan is innocent. She also knows Megan is great at what she does. It's not Megan she's mad at. It's her husband. It's this damn leadership job - a job she never even wanted in the first place. It's her situation in life.

Flustered, Tricia grasps for reasons.

"You're dismissive of protocol. You undermine my authority. You...you...you spend too much time talking to co-workers."

Megan is exacerbated. "Too much time with co-workers? Jesus, Tricia, why do you hate me so much?"

Tricia is cornered, on the ropes, and she knows it. Her voice begins to quiver.

"Everyone laughs at your jokes. They invite you to have drinks. People make space for you at their table. I eat alone. *Every single night!* You'd think just once you could come home for dinner?! Is that too much to ask?! Huh?! Is it?!"

Megan looks at Davey. "What the hell is she talking about?" He shrugs, his eyes wide with excitement, furiously chewing his carrot sticks like popcorn at the movies.

Tricia is unraveling. Then it all comes spilling out.

"The patients like you. The staff likes you. *Everybody* likes you! Why doesn't anyone like me?"

Tricia turns to Davey, pleading. "Why don't you like me?"

"Don't look at me," says Davey, holding up a hand as if to block her. "I'm into dudes."

Tricia is a complete mess now. "*I'm* compassionate. *I'm* hard working. *I'm* well respected. *I'm* the one who is supposed to get this year's Compassion Award. *Me!*"

After a few moments, Tricia collects herself, trying to regain some semblance of dignity and composure.

Megan finally speaks. "You know what, Tricia? I used to be afraid I'd end up alone. But I'm more afraid that I'll end up like you."

Megan turns to leave, but not before Tricia fires one last volley in her direction.

"Well, at least I'm married. Bitch."

Davey gasps "Oh shit," and throws a hand over his mouth.   Megan stops dead in her tracks. Fists clenched, she turns to face her smug, pale, unhappily married supervisor. She looks to Davey, as if seeking his approval. His look says it all. Go for it. With one mighty windup, Southie-tough Megan swings. *BOOM!* Tricia grabs a bloodied nose.

"Yahtzee!" yells Dave looking for a high-five.

The doors burst open. Loretta rushes into the room.

"Megan, come quick. It's Jackie Boy. He's at the Carney!"

CARNEY HOSPITAL – DORCHESTER

If you're Irish, from Southie, and sick, then the Carney is the only Emergency Room you let them take you. Chances are, you're going to be related to someone on staff and they'll move you up the pecking order.

Megan stands over her father as he lies in the hospital bed.

"Dad? Dad, can you hear me?" she whispers.

Jackie stirs. "Megan? Megan, is that you? All I see is a bright light."

He opens his eyes and gives her a wink. She punches him, relieved, then throws her arms around his neck, hugging him close. As much as Jackie Boy drives her crazy, Megan couldn't bear the thought of losing her father.

"Got a little nervous when I saw a hospice nurse standing over me," says Jackie, still tight in his daughter's embrace.

"What happened?" she asks.

"Promise you won't be mad," he says negotiating like a child, refusing to raise his eyes to meet hers.

"Let me hear it first and then I'll decide," she replies suspiciously.

Jackie's story will have to wait. Davey and Loretta roll into the room with a wheelchair. "Your ride's here, big guy," chirps Davey.

"How's Tricia doing?" Megan asks.

"She had it coming, the way she treats you," replies Davey. "Besides, you finally put some color in her face."

Jackie Boy looks lost. "What happened?"

"Your Southie Princess here smacked Tricia on the nose," Davey tells him.

"Really? That's my girl," cheers Jackie Boy. "Oorah!".

"Stop it. I feel terrible," says Megan genuinely ashamed of her Irish temper.

"She's got bigger problems than a bloody nose," says Loretta. "That 'procurement' investigation? Tricia's the one who's been stealing meds."

"And using *your* PIN code," adds Davey with punctuation.

"That *bitch*," sneers Megan, finally finishing the word.

Davey explains. (He *loves* being the one in the know for any and all kinds of juicy gossip.)

"After your little Southie boxing match, Trishie scurried off. I went to see if she was OK and found her in the dispensary. Seemed weird. So, I had my friend Jerry check it out - you know, the cute guy in I.T.? He matched her barcode and PIN strokes to the surveillance video."

"Tricia forgot there was a camera in there," adds Loretta.

"More like, she forgot that us gays are *everywhere*, and 'The Velvet Mafia' see *everything*," chirps Davey.

Megan is confused. "I don't understand. Tricia's taking drugs?"

"They're not for her," Loretta confirms. "They're for Edward."

Davey pipes up. "Poor man. Drugged and in the closet all these years. A closet full of 'Lane Bryant' clothes and 'Payless' shoes. Can you imagine?!"

Loretta looks directly at Megan. "I guess she's just afraid of being alone."

Megan nods. The words are not lost on their intended target.

There's a knock and everyone turns to see Tim Wallace standing by the door carrying Jackie's tire, weight belt and chain.

"Awe, shit," grumbles Jackie Boy sliding down and pulling the sheet over his head.

"Is it that bad?" asks Tim, looking around innocently. "I didn't think he needed a hospice nurse."

"This is my father," declares Megan, totally confused. "What? What are you doing here?"

Megan glares at Jackie Boy now hiding under the covers like a child. "Can somebody please tell me what happened?!"

Tim does his best to explain. "I was biking my route through Castle Island and heard a scream, so I rushed over and found your father lying on the ground."

Jackie peaks out from under the covers.

Megan snaps at him. "I told you to stop dragging that stupid tire around. You threw your back out again, didn't you?!"

"It's not my back," growls Jackie Boy from under the sheet.

"Then why were you on the ground?" she asks. Jackie Boy doesn't answer. He doesn't want to.

Megan waits, still glaring. Marines do not retreat unless that retreat will lead to victory. But at this moment, Jackie Boy would like nothing other than to jump out of bed, turn high tail and get the hell out of the room.

Out of excuses, he pulls the sheet down and blurts, "I was feeding the squirrels, OK?! Ungrateful little bastard bit me. Eight Rabies shots! Worse than the time I went to Bangkok."

Davey and Loretta try not to laugh. Megan is pissed.

"I figured he should get checked out," says Tim still holding the tire and chain. "They wouldn't take his stuff in the ambulance, so I offered to ride it over."

With that, Tim swings the tire onto a chair and - CRASH! A bag of seeds and nuts spill to the floor.

All eyes are on Jackie. Davey and Loretta finally bust with laughter.

"I'll have you know, that bag of seed can weigh up to 20 pounds," Jackie says trying to impress. They aren't.

"Pulling squirrel food in a tire?" cries Loretta through the laughter. "I better warn Michael that's how they train in the Corps."

They are all laughing now. Everyone except Jackie Boy. And Tim. Tim is doing his best to stay serious and make a good impression on Jackie Boy.

"Megan told me you used to be a Marine," he says.

"*He is a Marine!*" yell Megan, Davey, and Loretta in spontaneous unison.

Jackie tries to regain his authority – and dignity. "Ok. At ease. That's the last time I try to do something nice," he says climbing into the wheelchair. "Get me outta here, will ya?"

Davey rubs his back. "Don't you worry, Jackie Baby. I'll come down to see you every day to help out."

Jackie rolls his eyes. "Good God. Get me a hospice nurse. I'm ready to die."

Loretta pushes the wheelchair. "I'll take Tarzan here home in my car. Got something I need to show him." She looks at Tim on the way out. "I'm sorry about your mother, sweetie."

"Thank you," Tim replies softly, then turns to face Megan. After a few moments, it's just the two of them- and it's uncomfortable. "Megan, I...I really need to talk with you," he says almost pleading for her to listen. But she doesn't want to hear it. She heads to the hall for the elevator. Tim chases after her.

The elevator doors open and Megan steps in.

"Megan, please..."

She holds up her hand. "Stop. Go home to your family, Tim. I need to be with mine."

The elevator doors close.

Tim is left standing there, devastated, and alone.

****

Megan stands in lobby of the Carney Hospital Emergency Department, noting the irony of being on the opposite side of a bustling nurses station. She quietly thinks to herself, 'Maybe I should have taken that promotion when it was offered. Nice office job. Normal hours. Jesus, first Masshole Joe was right, then Jackie Boy.'

It's been that kind of a week.

But Megan declined the Board's offer, and instead recommended Tricia, thinking the leadership role would be good for her. It might make Tricia happy. Soften her a bit.

Megan now realizes, that's not working out so well.

God knows Megan could use the extra money the promotion would have provided. That Marine Corps dedication coursing through her bloodstream, mixed with good old-fashioned Irish-Catholic guilt has been making her reach into her own pocket for outlier patients in need like the Lopez family. She wasn't about to just stand by and do nothing. Screw protocol and rules and bank accounts.

But, Megan wanted to stay with the patients at their bedside. Listening. Caring. Comforting. She *needed* to be there - so they would never be alone.

And, well, she realizes, that's not working out so well either.

She walks over to a sliding glass window and mindlessly takes the discharge papers from a friendly nurse.

"Is someone bringing your car around?" asks the nurse.

"Excuse me?" says Megan.

"Are you alone?" the nurse replies.

The words echo and swirl around Megan's head. She doesn't answer, just looks to the Emergency Contact papers in her hand that read:

RELATIONSHIP TO PATIENT - PLEASE CHECK ONE:

There's a commotion behind her near the exit. Megan looks to the street to see Loretta and Davey trying to help Jackie Boy into the car. Flailing his arms. Yelling. Acting like a petulant child. "I don't need any help!" she hears Jackie bark.

Megan smiles at the three of them. Maybe her life isn't the one she'd imagined. Husband. Kids. House in the suburbs. Soccer games and PTA meetings. But for her, right now, at this moment, it's perfect.

She checks all four boxes on the form.

X̲ **PARENT**

X̲ **CHILD**

X̲ **SPOUSE**

X̲ **FRIEND**

"No," Megan replies proudly, as if to herself. "I'm not alone."

She hands the forms back and asks the nurse, "Did you see a gentleman go by here? Brown hair. Gray sweatshirt. He may have had a bike with him?"

"You mean Tim Wallace?" the nurse replies knowingly.

"You know him?"

"Well I should. I see him every day," she says.

The nurse points to a large family portrait in the adjacent lobby of Tim with his wife Laura, and their daughter Olivia. It hangs above an architect's model of a gleaming new building. **The Genevieve Wallace Cancer Center**.

Beside the plastic model is a television playing a video loop of the construction plans. Tim Wallace, founder and CEO of DIGITRON, is being interviewed on screen. He looks professional and all business in a dark suit and tie.

"Our goal with this new facility is to provide people anything they need, regardless of their ability to pay. At their most vulnerable, no one should have to worry about finances or medicine or medical supplies. We want to help people cross peacefully. Dignified. On their terms."

"That was a pretty exceptional donation," says the hospital spokesperson interviewing Tim on screen.

Tim thinks before speaking. "Well, a great man once said 'There's nothing exceptional or noble in being philanthropic. It's the other attitude that confuses me.'"

Megan is watching, mesmerized. "Oh my God," she whispers aloud. "Paul Newman."

"Excuse me?" asks the nurse who is now standing beside her, intrigued.

"It was Paul Newman who said that," says Megan, staring blankly at the screen.

The video begins to show Tim with his wife and daughter, smiling, shovels in hand, at the groundbreaking ceremonies.

"Did you know the family?" the nurse asks. But Megan is trying to process it all.

"What? Yes. Ah, no. No, I didn't," Megan stammers, dumbstruck, trying to take it all in.

"Such a tragedy," the nurse begins sadly. "I was on the floor that night. Drunk driver. They were already gone by the time EMS got them here."

She turns to face Megan. "Do you want me to go find Mr. Wallace for you? Miss?"

But Megan has already walked away.

(courtesy of larry richardson)

SOUTH BOSTON

Jackie Boy Hayes was never one to be intimidated. In fact, there are few people in his life that even made him nervous. He was nervous around Polly when they first dated. He was nervous in front of Dicka Finn when he had to perform the Marine Crucible test.* But, that was just his nerves. Truth be told, Jackie Boy was always been a little uncomfortable around strong women. But he is absolutely scared shitless of Loretta Evans.

He sits up straight in the front seat of Loretta's sparkling red BMW. Along with being sassy, comfortable in her sense of self, and giving zero fucks, Loretta is crazy rich since she divorced no-good husband Carl and took every penny of his multi-chain dry cleaning business. Karma is truly a bitch.

The dashboard of her car is covered in religious paraphernalia. Crucifix. Prayers cards. A medallion of the Virgin Mary dangles from the rear-view mirror. It's like some sort of four-wheeled Vatican City - if the Pope drove a sparkling red BMW.

Loretta drives slow - painfully slow. Life goes at *her* pace, not the other way around. 'It's the way God intended it,' she tells people. Life according to Loretta Evans.

She keeps glancing over in Jackie's direction, the contempt between them is like a third passenger in the front seat.

"Let me guess," she says noticing his look of disdain at the makeshift Vatican dashboard display. "You're not a religious man."

"Never saw the point, Ma'am," replies Jackie Boy. "Bullets find Bible-praying Catholics just as easily as they find the Atheists"

"Is that so," Loretta says. "You pray?"

"No."

"Believe in Jesus?"

"I believe in Corps and country," Jackie Boy states proudly.

"You need to believe in something bigger than yourself, Captain Hayes," she tells him. They both stare at the road ahead as cars rush past in a hiss of wet pavement.

Loretta breaks the silence. "I just hope Michael signs up because he wants to, not because he thinks he's out of options."

Jackie waits a second before stating, "Not everyone who joins the military is confused."

"And not everyone who prays to God is lost," Loretta quickly replies. There's a long pause as the two eye each other up and down, as if there's a new-found respect between them.

After a minute, Jackie says, "I coulda just taken the bus home, Ma'am."

"You'd never make it without getting kicked off," Loretta shoots back, full of her usual sass. "And stop calling me Ma'am. I'm younger than you. It creeps me out."

"Yes, Ma'am. I mean, Roger that," Jackie says and looks out the passenger window. "This isn't the way home."

Loretta turns to him with had a wide mischievous grin, and says, "I know."

(* The Crucible is a test every recruit must go through to become a Marine. It tests them physically, mentally and morally and is the defining experience of training. It takes place over 54-hours and includes food and sleep deprivation and over 45 miles of marching.)

****

Loretta's car stops at the edge of Castle Island. Jackie steps out of the BMW and slowly walks toward the Lieutenant Colonel Richard Finn Memorial. There, standing at attention beside the stone, is Michael Evans holding a rigid salute as if he were the assigned guard watching over the Tomb of the Unknown Soldier.

Jackie Boy looks around, shaking his head in stunned disbelief. The area is spotless. The spray paint removed. The brass plaque is polished and gleams in the sunlight. It is all beautiful.

"Commendable job, soldier," says Jackie Boy, truly moved. "Commendable job, indeed."

Jackie takes a moment to absorb the change to the memorial, and the change to the boy standing in front of him. He gives Michael a warm paternal smile.

Then, collecting himself, Jackie Boy steps back and snaps a flawless military salute. Michael snaps one back in form as the two soldiers, the two *friends*, stand side by side as the sun begins to set over the Lieutenant Colonel Richard Finn Memorial.

GIORDANO HOUSE - EAST BOSTON

Megan enters the front door with an empty lasagna tray in hand. Since the suspension for slugging Tricia, she's not wearing her typical nursing scrubs. She looks different in her street clothes. More relaxed and pretty.

The house is quiet. Unusually quiet. No arguing. No yelling. No noise at all. Megan heads up the stairs to Mrs. Giordano's room. It is empty, and the bed is gone.

Megan makes her way down the stairs and stops when she sees the Giordano boys standing beside their mother. In her bed. In her kitchen.

Mrs. Giordano has crossed over. And like Mrs. Wallace, Mr. Lopez, and her own mother before them, Megan wasn't there – for any of them - and she's beginning to realize, that's ok.

Bruno looks up and speaks softly. "We moved her, so she could spend her last few hours in the place she loved best, surrounded by the sounds and smells she loved the most."

Megan smiles at the tender gesture. "You boys did this all by yourself?"

"We hardly yelled once," boasts Marco with pride.

"Ma was tough," says Silvio, fighting back tears. "I think she hung in there just to make sure we were gonna be alright without her."

"You will be," Megan assures them. And she means it.

"You think we should say a prayer maybe?" asks Stevie.

"You know any?" says Silvio.

"I know some," replies Bruno.

"Yo, Father Guido Sarducci over here," snaps Marco.

"Who are you, the Pope?" says Bruno.

"I know more lines than you do!" yells Stevie.

"Boys, boys. Stop. This..." intervenes Megan. But then she stops herself, and smiles. "This would make your mother very happy."

They bow their heads.

Marco tries first. "Our Father who art in heaven, hallowed be thy name...and to the republic for which it stands..."

He's lost and looks to his feet. Now it's Bruno's turn.

"Hail Mary full of Grace the Lord is with thee..."

The brothers chime in.

"Blessed art thou amongst women and blessed is the fruit of..of...."

Lost again. Each one of the boys tries to finish.

"One nation under God."

"The baby Jesus."

"The loom."

"With liberty and justice for all."

They're all stumped.

Megan holds up a hand for them to stop. It's a gesture that says, 'I got this, boys.'

Then, Megan finds something that's been hidden inside her — it's a calmness and sudden peace that manifests itself in words that have been buried for years. She speaks softly and with resolve, as if soothing something restless in her soul.

Megan Hayes, hospice nurse, Southie tough daughter and friend, bows her head, folds her hands, and begins to pray.

"*Almighty Father, whose command is over all and whose love never fails, make me aware of Thy presence and obedient to Thy will. Keep me true to my best self, helping me to live so that I can face my loved ones and Thee without shame or fear. If I am tempted, make me strong to resist. If I should miss the mark, give me courage to try again.*"

With conviction and new-found strength, Megan says the final words. "*If I am inclined to doubt, steady my faith.*" *

Bruno whispers out the side of his mouth, "Nice prayer. Apostles?"

Megan replies firmly, proudly. "Marines."

(*the Marine Corp prayer)

HAYES HOUSE - SOUTH BOSTON

Jackie Boy sits at the kitchen table scanning the Help Wanted Ads in the Boston Herald. The back-door swings open. Megan walks in and tosses a stuffed animal toy squirrel onto the counter. Ever since he got home from the hospital, Jackie has been getting barraged with squirrel jokes. Megan's gift falls alongside an assortment squirrel paraphernalia; Rocky and Bullwinkle dolls. Squirrel Nut candies. Bags of seeds.

"N.G. wanted me to give you that," she tells him.

"Well at least it's not squirrel Chow Mein," growls Jackie. "Go put all this stuff in my room, will ya?"

"Why can't you?" she replies. After a moment she realizes something. "There aren't any squirrels in your room, Dad. I checked."

"I'm not afraid of squirrels!" he barks. "You looked in the closet, right?"

"Yes, Dad, I checked the closet," she says, trying to be patient since he asks her to check the closet every single day. For a tough, hardened Marine, Jackie Boy, is terrified of strong women, Loretta Evans - and now squirrels.

"Here, I got you something," Megan says, and slides an application in front of him.

"That better not be for Walmart," he growls.

Megan joins her father at the kitchen table.

"Planet Fitness. No more pulling tires," she says and looks directly at him, because this is important. "You've been fighting a war, some invisible enemy chained to a tire ever since mom died." After a moment she adds, "we both have."

He knows she's right. Jackie Boy wore his wife's memory like a chain, and it carried him like a prisoner around the cold sidewalks of South Boston.

They sit in silence and Jackie notices how tired and sad his daughter looks. Morale is low, so he attempts to remedy the situation.

"You want to know the day I was most proud?" he asks.

"The day Davey asked you to walk him down the aisle?" Megan replies sarcastically.

"Very funny. You're close though," says Jackie. "It was that day you almost beat the crap out of Jimmy Burke."

Megan snorts a laugh. "Dinky little runt."

Jackie continues. "You were tough, and you were fearless, and you stood up for a friend."

Megan nods, remembering how much Davey appreciated her gesture that day in seventh grade.

"But that's not the thing I was most proud of," he says warmly, "I was proud that I had a daughter."

Jackie leans forward in his seat and tenderly takes his daughter by the hand.

"You know what Ronald Reagan said about the Corps? He said, 'some people spend an entire lifetime wondering if they made a difference in the world. The Marines don't have that problem.'"

Jackie Boy pauses for the proper effect. "I'd say the same thing goes for nurses."

Megan smiles. They're going to be alright.

MRS. WALLACE ROOM - QUINCY, MA

Tim Wallace stands alone in his mother's room staring blankly at the empty, non-electric bed. Megan enters and stops in her tracks when she sees him.

"Sorry, I...I didn't expect you..." she stammers, looking around the room. "I think I left my hat."

"I needed to get the karaoke machine," Tim replies, looking around the room as well. It's uncomfortable. They're both trying too hard, and it's obvious.

"Yeah, well, you never know when you're gonna want to break into a Barry White song," says Megan trying to break the tension. She finally looks at him. "I know about your family, Tim. I'm so sorry."

Tim pauses, almost relieved to finally have the truth out there. He turns and looks to the framed photo of his wife and daughter on his mother's nightstand.

"I was supposed to drive that night, but I was working...I was always working," he says, his voice full of regret.

"Conference calls. Business trips. Board meetings. 'You're no fun anymore.' That's what Laura used to say to me."

He lifts his head toward Megan as if to seek forgiveness. "They had each other. They didn't die alone, right?"

"No Tim, they didn't die alone," says Megan with conviction. "No one does."

"I tried to tell you, but it just got easier for me to keep lying. To my mother. To myself. And the longer I kept it up, the more it felt like they never left."

"I understand," she replies.

"Their voices are still on my answering machine. I get to listen to them every night," he says with a sad smile. Then Tim pauses, reflecting. "I'm sorry Megan. I didn't want my mother to think I was alone. You just came into a lie that she needed. A lie that *I* needed."

He begins to twist at the wedding ring on his finger.

"I take this off every now and then. I'm not really sure what to do with it. I know it was wrong but..." his voice trails off. Then, he looks up, reaches over and takes Megan by the hand. "I can't lose someone else."

Megan's unsure how to react.

"You're not interested in me, Tim. You just think you like the nurse who took care of your mother."

He abruptly lets go of her hand.

"Maybe you're right," he says, and looks away. "How could I possibly fall for a girl who can kick my ass in puck bowling? You don't do beer funnels. You suck at ice luges. You can't even ride a bike for crying out loud."

Megan is a bit stunned. 'Shit,' she thinks to herself, 'what did I just do?'

Then suddenly, Tim grabs her by the waist and pulls her in close. "But I will tell you this. I could *absolutely* fall for the girl who punched out Tricia."

Megan smiles. It's the wide, pleasant smile of a girl falling in love, and one that Tim has never seen on Megan's face. And it makes him smile too.

They are about to kiss, but Megan kiddingly stops him with both hands on his chest.

"You, ah, you don't own any blue silk shirts, do you?"

CASTLE ISLAND

It's springtime in South Boston.

Lush green grass blankets the park landscape and colorful flowers bloom as people begin their morning exercise rituals. Women in Lycra running outfits stretch against a park bench. A group of cyclists in Spandex remove bikes from the top of their Prius. A chain is wrapped around a car tire. A worn leather weight belt is strapped around a waist.

Head down, tire in tow, a trim and confident Michael Evans slowly jogs along the edge of Boston Harbor. His focus never wavers.

He doesn't see the cyclists. He doesn't see the joggers.   He doesn't see overweight Private Investigator Charlie Peters slowly lumbering towards him in his own attempt to jog, sweating profusely from his freshly shaven head now that the mud flap combover has been mercifully removed.

ROXBURY

Santiago Lopez sits in the Roxbury Community Center classroom. The chair is ill-equipped to accommodate his large frame. A teacher looks on proudly works on reading the words from a book on the desk.

He turns his head to look out the window, and smiles. All the trees are full of life, dressed in their beautiful green bloom.

EAST BOSTON

The Giordano boys prepare dinner for their father Angelo.

A long table is overflowing with antipasto, baked eggplant, three kinds of pasta, chicken parmigiana and bread. Lots and lots of bread. Just another Tuesday night supper at the Giordano house.

They cook and argue and eat and argue. It's the Italian soundtrack. The music of the house.

HOSPITAL

A bow-tied, nebbish looking Doctor tenderly holds his fingers and thumb to the sides of Tricia's once-broken nose. It's healing nicely since her 'Southie boxing match' with Megan. The doctor smiles. He likes what he sees. So does Tricia. There's clearly a spark between them.

Tricia notices he has no wedding ring. How convenient. Her ring has been removed ever since the formal separation from Edward.

SOUTH BOSTON

Jackie Boy yells toward Megan's room.

"Let's move, Missy. Double time! We need to jettison and be in position at 1330 hours."

"You got everything?" Megan yells to him back through the bedroom door.

"Affirmative!" he barks.

Megan stares at her reflection in the mirror and likes what she sees - so much more than the cold winter bus stop reflection. New hairdo. New makeup. New Megan.

Jackie Boy opens the door to her bedroom and stands in stunned silence at the sight of his daughter wearing the white flowing wedding dress that his bride Polly wore.

"You look beautiful," he says choking back tears. "Just like your mother."

He collects himself and tugs at his uniform.

"Still fits," he grins with pride.

Megan approaches her father and adjusts the brim of his white military cap.

"John Donald 'Jackie Boy' Hayes, you *are* one handsome Marine."

Jackie smiles, a deep caring smile of love and of pride and of fatherhood.

"Semper Fi, little girl."

"Always, Daddy," she smiles. "Always."

OLD SOUTH CHURCH

At the grand, gothic entrance of the church stands Jackie Boy Hayes dressed sharp in his Marine Dress Blues. Only this time, he is the one absolutely beaming. Beside him stands Megan, stunning in her flowing wedding dress.

Organ music echoes about the heavenly vaulted ceilings as father and daughter slowly begin to walk down the aisle.

Davey cries on Kevin's shoulder.

Loretta sits with Michael and smiles proudly. As father and daughter approach, Michael gives Jackie Boy a big thumbs up. Jackie smiles back.

They approach the alter. Jackie Boy kisses his daughter tenderly on the cheek then turns to Tim.

"Don't screw this up, kid."

Tim gives him a confident, 'Megan-like' cocky smirk, and says, "I got this."

Tim takes Megan by the hand. The organ music stops. Megan looks to Tim, confused. She turns and looks up at the balcony to see a large Gospel choir high above the congregation.

Swaying in unison, they begin a soulful choral
rendition of MY EVERYTHING by Barry White;

I know there's only, only one like you
There's no way they could have made two
You're all I'm living for, your love I'll keep forevermore
You're the first, the last, my everything

"Are you crazy?" says Megan, tears of joy in her eyes.
"Sing a Barry White song at the Old South Church?!"

Tim shrugs, "You wouldn't let me finish at
Murphy's," and smiles, his trademark boyish smile with a
dimple, the same one that Megan fell in love with the very
first time she saw him in his Hawaiian shirt and straw hat.

EPILOGUE

Military drums roll as Jackie Boy stands at attention reviewing his look in the mirror.

He pulls out a pair of clean white gloves from the top drawer of his dresser, fitting them snugly on each finger.

He aligns his belt and rubs his thumb over a smudge on his spit polished black shoes.

He sets a white military cap firmly on his head.

Checking his appearance in the mirror, he brushes a single fallen hair off his shoulder.

In the long tradition of brave Marines who fought at Iwo Jima, Guadalcanal, Okinawa, and Khe San, Jackie Boy Hayes is preparing for the toughest, most perilous battle of his life.

He leans in close to the mirror, takes a deep breath, exhales, and says, "I got this."

****

A tumbling herd of schoolchildren come running down the street towards their elementary school, pushing and shoving their way to the crosswalk.

A proud 68-year-old Marine in full Dress Blue uniform steps from the curb and out into the street. With a crisp white-gloved hand held high, he yells "Halt!"

The kids stop in their tracks.

"TEN HUT!" he barks. The kids snap to attention.

Jackie Boy begins to inspect his miniature 'troops', walking up and down the line of his new recruits, pointing out imperfections as each child reacts in order:

"Laces."

The laces get tied.

"Gum."

The gum is spit out.

"Bangs."

A freckled face girl with pigtails and a missing front tooth doesn't react.

Jackie repeats his order. "Bangs."

Still nothing. He bends to face the little girl.

"What's your name soldier?"

"Katie," she says proudly, as if Jackie (and everybody) should know.

"Well, *Katie*, your bangs need to be brushed aside."

"No," snaps Katie, full of piss and vinegar.

Jackie raises an eyebrow, impressed with her confidence and bravado.

"No, huh?"

Katie shakes her head defiantly. She's not budging on this bangs thing.

An attractive woman around Jackie's age approaches from behind. "I'm sorry about this one,'" she says, out of breath from chasing Katie. "She can be really tough."

"Yeah," says Jackie Boy, noticing the little girl's clenched right fist. "I know the type."

Katie breaks formation and tugs at the woman's long plaid skirt.

"See Grandma," she says, pointing up at Jackie Boy. "This is the man I was telling you about. Doesn't he look like he used to be a Marine."

Grandma reviews Jackie up and down, and likes what she sees.

"Oh no, sweetie," replies the attractive older woman in a flirty voice. "This *is* a Marine."

John Donald 'Jackie Boy' Hayes, defender in battle, a Marine's Marine, a soldier who represents fearlessness and bravery and relentless drive - turns bright red and weak at the knees.

Jackie Boy snaps out of it, and turns his attention back to the 'troops,' marching his charge of children with fine military precision through the yellow lined crosswalk.

He bellows in cadence as the kids yell back in unison.

Mama Mama don't you cry/ Mama Mama don't you cry.

The Marine Corps motto is Semper Fi/ The Marine Corps motto is Semper Fi

The kids now safely on the other side, Jackie chants, *"One, two, three, four. United States Marine Corp!"*

The miniature Marines cheer back, *"Oorah!"*

Shoulders back, eyes straight, Jackie Boy Hayes snaps a flawless military salute, and grins wide from ear to ear.

****

From the Halls of Montezuma

To the Shores of Tripoli;

We will fight our country's battles

In the air, on land and sea;

First to fight for right and freedom

And to keep our honor clean;

We are proud to claim the title

Of United States Marine.

RIP Steve Bowen

1942-2016

ACKNOWLEDGMENTS

To Captain Donald Hayes, USMC, Ret., who taught me there is no such thing as a former Marine.

Oorah and Semper Fi!

Amanda Carnes, RN, BSN Boston Children's Hospital, Dana-Farber Cancer Institute's Jimmy Fund Clinic, Hole-in-the-Wall Gang Camp Counselor.

Neighbors. Friends. Inspirations.

Thank you to Dawn Wolfrom who found my screenplays.

And a special thank you to Cayman Grant who encouraged my writing and helped me shape my stories.

I am forever grateful.

Amanda Carnes, Don Hayes, Mike Bernard

Retired Marine puts on dress blues to act as crossing guard for Pennsylvania kids

From the halls of Montezuma to the crosswalks of Lancaster, PA

Retired Marine Cpl. Lewis Alston, 63, decided to take matters into his own hands when he saw that schoolchildren near his home were endangered by heavy traffic while walking to class. "I saw, when I was coming down the street, a student that ran in between the cars," Alston told <u>ABC News</u>. "The traffic will not stop for the children at all."

When school started this week, the retired Marine thought it would be helpful, if not cool, to put on his dress uniform and shepherd students across a busy intersection leading to Martin Luther King, Jr. Elementary School. "Wouldn't it be a golden opportunity for the students to see a Marine help them cross the street?" he said.

Other streets near the school have crossing guards, but limited city resources have left Alston's busy corner unguarded. So, each week day morning and afternoon, he buttons up his corporal's dress blues, slips on his white gloves and snaps on his hat. The kids love it, Alston said. "They say, 'Thank you, sir,'" the Vietnam vet recalled proudly.

And he snapped a perfect military salute and went back to his charges.

reprinted from New York Daily News Aug 28, 2014 Deborah Hastings

Also by Mike Bernard

A FISHERMAN'S VIEW

After their mother's death, colorful Irish patriarch Michaleen Fitzgerald gives his estranged children three plastic baggies – RED, GREEN, YELLOW - to scatter her ashes at specific locations. The symbolism is not lost on them. Theresa is the angry one, Richard is materialistic, and Fiona is crippled with anxieties. But they're wrong. The colors represent something else entirely, and the journey to dispose the ashes and find their true meanings and destinations has just begun.

With dark but tender humor, Michaleen helps his children take a different view of life, hoping they'll grab it by the lapels and swing it back onto the dance floor, but each child is harboring complicated feelings and secrets that threaten to tear their family apart.

A FISHERMAN'S VIEW is a deeply emotional story of reconciliation and a celebration of family; how people who were raised so close can be so far apart without truly knowing it.

Available on Amazon.com

FACEBOOK: @afishermansview

ABOUT THE AUTHOR

Mike Bernard is the founder of ChathamPoint Group, an executive search firm outside Boston. His 'midlife crisis' writing career began when his children and his money went off to college - checks made out to Loyola University Maryland (x2) and Assumption College respectively. Mike's work has placed in the NICHOLL FELLOWSHIP, BLUECAT, FINAL DRAFT Big Break and PAGE International screenplay competitions. Three of his screenplays were optioned and under development with production companies.

Mike is a graduate of Providence College and Boston College High School. He resides in Medfield, MA with his wife Michele. He spends summers on the beaches of Cape Cod and winters roaming the aisles of Home Depot.

Comments, questions please contact:
meb123@comcast.net

Made in the USA
Middletown, DE
14 July 2019